The Prodigal Renegade

The Prodigal Renegade

Time is not a friend when there is no loyalty except yours.

Victor Fakunle

Alive Book Publishing

Additional copies may be ordered from the publisher for educational,
business, promotional or premium use.
For information, contact ALIVE Book Publishing at:
alivebookpublishing.com, or call (925) 837-7303.

Book Design by Alex Johnson

ISBN 13
978-1-63132-069-9

ISBN 10
1-63132-069-6

Library of Congress Control Number: 2019941293

Library of Congress Cataloging-in-Publication Data
is available upon request.

First Edition

Published in the United States of America by ALIVE Book Publishing
and ALIVE Publishing Group, imprints of Advanced Publishing LLC
3200 A Danville Blvd., Suite 204, Alamo, California 94507
alivebookpublishing.com

PRINTED IN THE UNITED STATES OF AMERICA

10 9 8 7 6 5 4 3 2 1

I sailed all the way with no reason

Wondering why the sway, where is my beacon?

Life seems all against, can this be the entire season?

Who can deny all the stains, I see a light in the horizon

Nevertheless, I was a prodigal renegade

Who knew that would be the reason I got saved

—Victor Fakunle

Acknowledgement

To the ONE who sits on the throne, in whom I live and exist, glory be to His name.

I would like to dedicate this book to my wonderful wife, Kristie Fakunle who has been by my side for the past eighteen years. I bless God for you in my life. Your love, and dedication to my success cannot be quantified. You are my rock. Thank you for loving me.

Writing this book has been a wonderful experience. Despite the desire to write, this book would not have been possible except for the love and counsel of my friend, Fidelis Odogbo who encouraged me to take the leap.

Much appreciation to my sister, Adeyinka Oyebanji who was relentless in her efforts and cheering me on till I finished the book.

Finally, my gratitude to my parents, my family and friends who have supported me in all my endeavors. God bless you all.

Chapter 1

JUST BEFORE NOON, HE ARRIVED at Muritala Mohammed International Airport in Lagos. Danny was once again in his homeland, after a ten-year hiatus to the United States. The buildings at the airport were just how Danny remembered them when he was young. Nothing much has changed. The row of houses with rusty water tanks in various colors on roof tops could still be seen a few yards away from the airport. Nostalgia overwhelmed him. As the plane taxied, he glared at the window notwithstanding the ache he felt from the handcuffs connected to his leg chains, since his departure from Pittsburg, Pennsylvania ten hours ago.

Everyone was eager to get off the plane. They stood and lined up, a learned behavior for men who had been incarcerated for years within a limited space, beckoning to get the next instruction from their task masters. Danny could not wait. He wondered what his dad would look like. Had he gained weight after all these years and how would he be received by the General? He needed some fresh air.

Danny could hear metal chains and handcuffs pilling up on the floor closer to the cockpit. The U.S. Marshal was a gray-haired white gentleman making sure all deportees exited the plane in a humane and presentable manner, paying respect to the family members waiting at the reception. Danny sighed and thanked God for the marshal. He had seen worse.

The smell in the airport was familiar. The moldy smell and the lack of great air ventilation system was amplified by the tropical heat. At airport reception, officers from the Nigeria Police and Immigration Service were visibly present to take some of the former inmates to Alagbon. During the roster call, Danny prayed. As a kid, he had heard of the notorious Alagbon Police Station at Ikoyi. Stories of torture, extortion and inhumane treatment of deportees sent chills into his bones. Despite Danny's experience at Petersburg Prison, he still wondered about his chances of survival in Nigeria. He heard his name called to the Immigration Service with great relief. He was grateful to God.

When the General arrived at the airport, Danny was delighted. He immediately prostrated.

"Good afternoon sir," said Danny avoiding eye contact.

"Hello Danny. How are you? Are you okay? Sorry for the delay. I got stuck in traffic. Did the officers treat you well?"

"Yes, they did, sir. I have no complaints."

"You look tired. I'm sure you are hungry. Your mum is at home cooking for you. Glad to have you back son."

"Me too, dad."

It was bright and sunny as they walked towards the car park. Danny stood still for a minute to feel the breeze and muttered beneath his breath, "Free at last".

12 YEARS EARLIER...

Chapter 2

JUST A FEW WEEKS AFTER DANNY'S SIXTEENTH BIRTH-
DAY, he took a stroll through the estate where his family had
lived since he was seven years old. Danny loved the Federal
Housing Estate and the Victoria Island neighborhood. The estate
was originally built by the Dutch as residential quarters for
members of the Nigerian House of Assembly and other senior
staffs of the legislative body. It was designated for Senior Staff
members of the Nigerian Civil Service. Evelyn worked at the
Ministry of Petroleum Resources. Though she was married to
the General, she raised Danny and his siblings almost as a single
mother. The General was always on postings.

Every day, Danny would strut though the estate, checking
out the beautiful girls chatting on the balconies of the high-rise
buildings. He loved the summer holidays, when most of his
friends were home from boarding school. One day, he noticed
Dexter waving his hands and signaling at him not to come home.
Dexter looked worried. He suddenly felt a knot in his stomach.
It was the same feeling he had on resumption day at boarding
school. Danny hated boarding school. He felt like a prisoner
when school was in session. The school was surrounded with
guards and high security barbed wires in the middle of the country sides of Kaduna State. The food was terrible. Danny felt the
knot in his stomach tighten. Just as it was in boarding school
when he did not have a choice and the odds were against him,
he decided to take his chances.

Danny climbed a flight of stairs to the third floor and met
Dexter at the entrance to the flat. Dexter's face spoke of despair,

confusion and pity for his elder brother. Dexter was three years younger and a computer savvy introvert.

"Dad is home and asked of you", Dexter whispered.

"What did you say?"

"I told him, I don't know, and he looked really pissed."

"Where is mum?" Danny asked.

"In the kitchen preparing dinner. I think Dad is going to kill you."

"The anticipation is killing me already," Danny replied.

Danny walked into the living room and saw the General sitting in his favorite chair facing the doorway. He immediately prostrated and said, "Good afternoon sir." The General was reading the newspapers and did not acknowledge his presence. Danny vanished into his bedroom, anticipating what was to come. He had seen this scenario play out before. The atmosphere was tense. Danny wondered if he would have the opportunity to choose his punishment.

A couple of weeks before, the General had called from his military post in Minna to speak to him. The phone rang, and Christy ran to pick it up before anyone else. She was Danny's baby sister and the General's favorite. She was born on the same day as he was and couldn't do any wrong. She chuckled constantly as the conversation went on, and finally she yelled, "Danny, Daddy wants to speak to you." For Danny, that was code for "Man, I'm in trouble." Hesitantly, he picked up the receiver and the General said, "Your mum told me you have been messing around with girls in the neighborhood and not studying for your exams. This is the second time you've failed your exams to graduate high school. I'm just giving you a heads-up. When I get home, I'm going to deal severely with you. Do you understand me?"

"Yes, I do sir," he replied. His father hung up. Danny was the first son and it was expected that he become either a doctor or an engineer. However, he did not share these interests with his

parents. He hated science but loved business and entrepreneur-
ial ventures.

Two weeks earlier, Evelyn had been in Danny's room looking
through his wardrobe. She felt a bulge in his coat pocket and
found 5000 naira in newly minted notes. Evelyn was at a loss for
words. It would take her three months to earn that much.

"Grace, Grace," she screamed as she ran to the flat next door.
Grace was Evelyn's neighbor. She had a knack for being in
everybody's business. Despite this, she was Evelyn's friend and
remarkably convenient.

Grace came out of her flat and asked, "What is the matter?"

"Look what I found in Danny's room. What's a fifteen-year-
old boy doing with 5000 Naira?"

Grace was not surprised. She had tried to tell Evelyn that
Danny was hanging out with some shady characters known for
trading mercury on the black market. The kids splurged on parties in night clubs, bought jewelry and hired limousines. She had
not had the courage to tell Evelyn.

"I don't know, but I think its time you told his dad before
things get out of hand".

While Danny was deep in thought, Uncle Boss came into the
room, looking perplexed and helpless. He had been designated
by the General to choose the tools for the execution. Uncle Boss
was Danny's first cousin, the son of his mum's sister. He had
come to live with them from the North to further his education.
Evelyn was his guardian and sponsor. He was the elder brother
Danny never had.

"Dad is calling you!" said Uncle Boss.

As Danny walked into the living room, he could see collec-
tion of whips had been assembled on the dinning table, arranged
by size. Danny could feel his heartbeat increasing and sweat running down his neckline.

"Sir, you requested for me?". Acting ignorant was the only
play left for Danny.

"Where were you?"

"I was in the bedroom, sir." I guess two can play this game of ignorance, Danny thought.

"Kneel down over there, raise your hands and close your eyes," the General said.

Danny followed orders without asking questions, just as the General expected from soldiers in his barracks.

Twenty minutes passed. There was no sound, except the television blasting out the voices of the NTA news anchor. The news broadcast was the most boring show on the planet, Danny thought. He liked to joke that if he grew up to work for the intelligence agency, he would make criminals listen to the news to get a guaranteed confession. Danny opened his right eye to take a peek. He suddenly felt a jolt on his thigh, hands and butt in very quick succession. The General was swift, and Danny held his hands to take a breath. This was the first time the General has enlisted his fist to guarantee a knockout. Now he knew what Ali had felt after couple of brutal punches from Joe Frazier, he thought.

Uncle Boss walked by and whispered, "You better run!" and to Danny's amazement, he heeded that advice. He jumped up and ran out into the streets without his shoes. Danny ran for miles through the estate, not giving a thought to the girls. He ran all the way to Chief's house and crashed into his living room.

After a glass of water, Danny explained to Chief what had transpired. Chief was not surprised. He had been bailing Danny out of trouble for a long time. Chief Ladi had been friends with the General since high school. He was a veteran public servant with the Nigerian Civil Service, just like Evelyn. He had studied in the United States for a while. Chief instructed Danny to wait at his residence, while he paid a visit to his dad to negotiate an end to the onslaught.

Danny was confident of Chief's diplomatic skills, especially when it was concerning his dad. The General had always had a soft spot for him and would grant him an audience no matter the situation. An hour later, Chief came home.

"I spoke to your dad and all is well. You can go back home. Just make sure to stay out of trouble."

"Sir, I don't want to go home, it's a trick," Danny said.

After much persuasion, he decided to go back home. Fortunately, he was not injured, except some minor friction burns on his feet. He tip-toed into his room and slept off with his right eye opened.

Chapter 3

DANNY WOKE UP IN THE MORNING, WONDERING IF THERE WOULD BE A SECOND BOUT of whipping. He contemplated a guarantee of his demise at the hands of the General by running through the glass door in the living room and hoping for death. He knew Evelyn would not have the grace to forgive him despite her Christian values. Uncle Boss walked into the room. Now, he was really irritated.

"Dad is calling you." As he walked into the living room, Danny could hear Evelyn crying uncontrollably in his parent's bedroom. The General was reading his newspaper with his usual poise, as if nothing had transpired the day before.

"Did you call for me, sir?"

"Yes, I did, he replied." Get your bags packed. You are moving out of this house to stay with your Uncle Jide."

That was unexpected. He still had to consider if suicide was still a better option.

Uncle Jide was the General's first cousin. A shrewd educator and a disciplinarian with a no-nonsense attitude. He lived at Fola-Agoro, a middle-class suburb on the outskirts of the slum of Bariga, on the east side of Lagos. Danny and his parents had visited Uncle Jide and his family often. A nostalgic feeling of boredom and uncertainty came over him. They had an old black & white television with an external antenna that reminded him of the Flintstones. The living room had lots of books on the shelves. This was not Danny's ideal escape, but it beats another bout with the General.

Danny and Evelyn arrived at Uncle Jide's flat later in the

evening. Evelyn was still sobbing. Danny had always hated seeing his mum cry. He felt a heavy burden of guilt and wished she was not there with him. Outside the flat was a sea of candles used by traders on the streets. The whole neighborhood was in darkness. This was not a surprise to Danny. The Nigerian Electric Power Authority was notorious in this regard. The lack of electricity for up to twenty hours a day was a common phenomenon, despite its officials harassing its customers for payment.

Aunt Kemi opened the door, knelt briefly and stood to embrace Evelyn. She was tall, beautiful and elegant, and the reason Danny had been able to endure his visits there. It was obvious that Uncle Jide was not home; it was hard to miss the old green Peugeot 504 with the plate number KDA4077 siting outside. It had belonged to the General when they lived in Kaduna. Uncle Jide had bought it a few years back from his dad and fixed it up.

Aunt Kemi eventually persuaded Evelyn to go home and assured her Danny was in good hands. It was late and getting dark.

Around ten o'clock, Danny heard some commotion in the living room. Finally, he heard Uncle Jide call his name.

"Danny, how are you?

"I'm fine, sir."

"Have you had dinner?" he asked.

"I'm not hungry, sir."

Uncle Jide was sitting in his favorite chair watching the NTA news channel, a habit he'd inherited from the General when he lived with them years ago before he got married.

"Talk to me," said Uncle Jide. "What is going on with you?" "Your dad called me and he is really disappointed in you."

That makes two of us, Danny thought.

"What do you want to do with your life?" Uncle Jide asked.

Danny was overwhelmed with emotions, tears rolling down his cheeks. He could not believe it. This is the first time anyone had asked his opinion. After gaining his composure, Danny decided to be upfront.

"I don't see myself in a lab coat, nor in a construction safety hat. I would love to study Social Science."

Uncle Jide smiled and motioned to his unpacked suitcase leaning in the door way. "Your room is ready, get some rest. You've had a long day."

Danny was surprised by the reception he got from the community of Fola-Agoro, especially the ladies. It had been two years since he'd been in the neighborhood, but he felt like he'd been there forever. It was a small community, and word got to the streets fast that a new kid had arrived from posh Victoria Island. Danny was happy to reap the benefits of people's assumptions. Everyone wanted to be Danny's friend and the feeling was mutual. He had always disliked the VI girls anyways. They were spoiled brats. In contrast, the people of Fola-Agoro were down-to-earth, hard-working straight shooters. Danny felt right at home.

One day a year later, Uncle Jide came home from work looking agitated. He had told Danny and Aunt Kemi that Danny's unofficial exam results would be ready before he left for work that morning. Danny had seen that expression before. Danny didn't mind getting sad news, but he wondered why he had to get it unofficially, two weeks ahead of his classmates. Uncle Jide went straight to his bedroom and Danny was left wondering if school was not his forte. Maybe I should consider vocational training as an auto mechanic, he thought.

Aunt kemi was gracious as always. Sweat poured down Danny's face even though the weather was cool.

"Don't worry, Danny. I'll check with your uncle and find out what is going on."

A few minutes later, she came out of the room with a big grin on her face and shook Danny's hand.

"You passed with flying colors," she said. Your uncle was

messing with you. Congratulations."

Goosebumps popped on Danny's arms. He felt suddenly cool, and gave a big smile.

Chapter 4

IT HAD BEEN SIX MONTHS SINCE THE OFFICIAL GCE RESULTS were released to the public. Danny's attitude changed. He strutted the streets like Tony Manero in *Staying Alive*. For the first time, Danny believed he was just as smart and book savvy as any other kid. He was ready to think about going to college, which he'd previously thought. An impossible feat.

The week before, Uncle Jide had suggested it was time to talk to the General about going back to VI. Danny shrugged off the idea. Why would he leave Fola-Agoro where he was treated like a king, just to return to be a regular Joe in VI? Danny had no intentions of ever returning home. Though he missed Dexter, Christy and Sade, that was not enough motivation to return to VI.

"Can I take a few days to think about it?" he asked. "I would just like to consider my options."

Uncle Jide agreed reluctantly. That would buy him some time to figure out his next move. At least, that's what he thought until he heard his mum's voice downstairs in the parking lot.

Evelyn walked in with a big grin on her face. She looked peaceful and rested. He was happy for her. It has not been easy for her, not having Danny home for the past two years. Though, he was in exile, Danny had returned home to VI when Uncle Jide and his family joined his family for a Christmas trip to the village. Danny was left home alone in Fola-Agoro. Evelyn had always left a spare key with the neighbors next door. Danny had a blast with his friends. He hadn't seen them for a while, but still had to be careful not to attract any attention to himself.

Danny became worried when he saw Chief Ladi walk into

the living room after Evelyn. He did not know what to make of his presence. Though Chief Ladi was a family friend and the General's confidante, it was no secret that Evelyn relied on Chief whenever she needed to make a decision the General might disagree with. Chief was a master negotiator and his presence spoke volumes. "This has to be good," Danny thought.

Danny could see Uncle Jide and his aunt were also curious to find out what was going on. After much pleasantries, Evelyn thanked both of them for their support and taking care of Danny.

"We are family. There is no need for that," said Uncle Jide. Evelyn glanced at Chief, and he took the cue.

"Danny will be going to the United States to further his studies."

What? Danny blurted out. He sat down with a puzzled look. For a minute, he could not feel his feet.

Uncle Jide sighed. "That's great news. That means Danny will be starting school as a freshman next year in August. Much time and opportunity to prepare."

"Danny leaves tomorrow night," said Evelyn.

"Tomorrow night?" Danny said.

"Actually, you are leaving with me and Chief immediately for VI. We need to pack and get ready. Go and get your stuff, we are waiting."

"How is this possible?" Uncle Jide said. "Danny will still have to apply for a visa and this could take couple of weeks".

"He already has a visa," Evelyn said. Everyone was puzzled.

"I must be dreaming," Danny muttered.

Danny could care less what he packed. He was excited beyond himself. He gave lots of hugs to his cousins and Aunt Kemi. Danny hated saying goodbye. He was going to miss his notoriety with the people of Fola-Agoro, especially the ladies. As he left with Evelyn and Chief, he felt himself getting teary-eyed.

They arrived late. It was around eleven o'clock. Evelyn had explained to Uncle Jide and Aunt Kemi the mystery of the United States visa and the sudden need to travel.

Two weeks ago, Evelyn had been cleaning up the bedroom and doing the laundry. The house had been in disarray because Christy had had a sleep over. She had been bugging Evelyn and the General for weeks to host her friends. This was a bold request that Danny and his siblings could not have dared to make when they were her age. As Evelyn rumbled through the drawers next to the bed, she stumbled on Danny's passport. She wondered why it was in the drawer instead of the family's safe where she kept all the important documents. She breezed through the pages and saw a U.S. B2 Visiting Visa for Danny that was valid for six months.

The nine o'clock news had just come on when Evelyn stormed into the living room and stood between the TV screen and the General.

"What is this? Can you explain how you got this?" She waved the passport in the General's face. Evelyn's posture was quite militant and determined. The General knew better than to aggravate her further. He sat up and explained.

For six weeks, a sect called Yan Tatsine had been terrorizing the residents of Kaduna State. The sect's actions were based on an Islamic extremist ideology. The group had attacked the U.S. Consulate in Kaduna and besieged the compound inhabited by the diplomats and the foreign service employees and their families. The General had been the Chief of General Staff at the 1st Mechanized Infantry Division in Kaduna. He had received the call to mobilize reinforcement to support the Nigerian Police and crush the rebellion. The operation was swift and successful. A couple of days later, the General received the U.S Consular-General and some high-ranking officials at the military headquarters. They were impressed and wanted to show their appreciation.

As the visiting delegation departed the headquarters, the Consular asked the General, if there was anything they could do for him personally? The General had to think fast and all he could think of was Danny. "Well, my son would like to go to the United States," he said. "Oh! That's not a problem, send his passport over to my office at the consulate and we will take care of that."

Two days later, Danny's passport was hand delivered to the General with a visa inside. By the time he arrived at the family home in Lagos for a weekend furlough, he'd begun to second-guess the idea. He locked the passport by the bedside drawer, lay down and dozed off thinking of his victory in Kaduna and what it might mean for his career.

Chapter 5

DANNY WOKE UP THE NEXT DAY IN HIS OLD BED, still reeling from the events of the day before. This has to be a dream, he thought. Evelyn came into his room to help him finish packing. Danny had never been to the U.S. All he knew about it was from the Hollywood movies and music videos. Though Evelyn had taken Danny and his siblings to Europe for vacation when they were younger, he knew the U.S. was totally different. Americans were very direct, which was his preferred style of communication. Danny was excited.

Nobody knew Danny was back in the estate. When they'd arrived, he'd wanted to share the good news with his friends. However, he couldn't shake from his mind the reason for his abrupt travel. Evelyn had been concerned about Danny telling his friends and getting into trouble. It wouldn't be the first time. He needed to play it cool and stay calm. He felt like he was being smuggled out of the country.

The flight was scheduled to depart from Muritala Mohammed Airport at 11:45pm and arrive at John F. Kennedy Airport in New York at 5:45am. Winter had just started on the East coast.

Evelyn had a three-piece suit dry cleaned for Danny. She wanted him looking sharp and responsible. Evelyn was putting her make-up on when the General arrived. He had been conveniently absent from the house through out the day. If he'd had his way, Danny would not be going to the U.S. Danny was immature and had the potential to get into trouble. But Evelyn had insisted that this kind of opportunity only comes once. She was convinced, especially now that Danny had passed his exams, that he would be okay. Eventually, the General gave up.

When the time came to go to the airport, Chief Ladi was sitting next to the General watching the news. He had come over to provide support for Evelyn and to be a mediator in case the General changed his mind. Danny could hear the horn of the car downstairs. Uncle Boss was being impatient and Danny was ready to get on with it. He went back to say goodbye to the General and Chief Ladi.

"Good bye, sir."

"Good bye," said General. "Watch out. Lots of people with HIV over there."

"The girls over there are very fair-skinned," Chief Ladi added with a grin. "You are going to like them."

"Thank you, sir." Danny took one last look at his home and ran out of the house before Uncle Boss took off without him.

THE AIRPORT WAS ROWDY AND CROWDED. Uncle Boss dropped them off at the departure lounge and drove off abruptly. Danny couldn't figure why Uncle Boss was in such a hurry to get back home. Maybe because he will finally have the room to himself again.

It took Evelyn and Danny over an hour to get to the check-in counter and go through security. Danny could see the plane from the lounge and got exited all over again. It was a Boeing 747. He'd only seen them in movies. Suddenly, an interruption by the voice from the overhead speakers.

"This is an announcement for passengers on Nigerian Airways, flight 334 departing for New York. Please proceed to gate D for boarding."

Evelyn got up and Danny followed. Thirty minutes later, the plane taxied to the runway for take-off. Danny was glued to the window looking at the homes next to the airport and a large billboard that read "Good-Bye to Nigeria". Danny muttered "goodbye". Twenty minutes later, it was pitch black outside and Danny was snoring.

DANNY'S EYES WERE STILL IRRITATED BY THE COLD when he got off the plane. He had never felt anything like it before. The coldest he'd ever been was in boarding school in Kaduna during the Harmattan season. A north-east trade wind blew dry and dusty particles from the Sahara Desert. Danny could remember how chapped his lips got and how his feet cracked open. He had learnt that Vaseline petroleum jelly could be a man's best friend.

"At least the heating system is working," said Danny. Evelyn ignored him and walked hastily through the airport lounge, to the baggage claim area. They had four bags each weighing exactly the maximum allowed by the airline. Evelyn had packed with precision, tact and skill. If she'd had her way, she would have brought more luggage, which would have been a major embarrassment for Danny. In the movies, Americans never had more than one bag. I'm going to act like an American, he thought. As they exited the terminal, all Danny could see was a sea of yellow taxis. Cars honked constantly. Pedestrians streamed along-side the cars. It was total chaos. This was just like Nigeria, except the officers and airport staff looked happy doing their jobs. Danny was accustomed to frowning at the airport in Lagos, to avoid unnecessary compliments and fake smiles from the officials expecting a tip.

"Can you take us to Penn Station?" Evelyn asked a taxi driver.

"Sure. Welcome to the United States," he said as he struggled to lift the luggage into the trunk of the car.

The taxi pulled up at the station around eight o'clock. Danny could not believe all the people sleeping on cardboard boxes and begging for a dollar. He had never seen that in the movies.

"We need to hurry up and catch the 9:00 a.m. Amtrak train

to New Carrolton, Maryland," Evelyn said. Their final destination was a secret Evelyn kept until now.

"Isn't that where Dele lives?" asked Danny.

"Yes. You will be staying with him and his guardian."

Danny was excited. He had not seen Dele, Chief Ladi's first son for over three years, since he'd graduated from high school. Dele and Danny had attended the same school and grown up in the estate together. Dele was a year ahead of Danny in school and was two years older. Despite their shared history, they were totally different people. Dele was an introvert and lacked Danny's charisma, especially with the girls at school. Dele had arrived in the U.S. immediately after his graduation. He had been born in Washington D.C, when Chief Ladi was studying for his master's degree. Danny's stomach growled. There was a McDonald's in the corner of the station. Danny glanced at it, then at Evelyn. Together they walked to the restaurant.

Chapter 6

I T'S ALMOST NOON WHEN THE TRAIN entered Prince Georges County. Danny had finished his double cheeseburger and large fries.

"Now it's official. I have arrived in the United States," said Danny. He had stayed up throughout the entire journey, enjoying the scenery. Danny saw huge stretch of farmlands and couple of horses grazing nearby. Most of the houses were beautiful with designs from the Victorian era. They reminded him of the colonial houses built by the British before Nigeria's independence. Evelyn was tired. She had slept through the trip and woken up to the voice of the train conductor announcing New Carrolton Station. She and Danny looked out the window and saw a short stocky man standing on the platform next to the ticket office grinning and waving.

"Welcome to New Carrolton madam. My name is Chubi," he said with a heavy Nigerian accent. "Chief Ladi gave me your itinerary and requested that I get here on time to meet you. How was your flight and the train ride?"

"Fine," said Evelyn as she tried to warm her cold hands by rubbing them together.

"This must be Danny. Heard a lot about you. Are you excited to be in the U.S.?"

"Yes, sir." Danny hoped whatever he had heard was good.

Together they walked to the parking lot. "Here we are," Chubi said, pointing to an eighties model Chevy Caprice station wagon with D.C taxi cab signage painted on the driver's side door. Danny jumped in the car. It was freezing. He could have cared less if it was a boat, so long it was warm.

The city felt quite different from the chaos in New York. Maryland had beautiful homes, lots of houses under construction in new residential developments. There were parks along the highway with kids playing on swings with young mothers pushing their strollers. It was a more relaxed and laid-back environment.

As Chubi pulled into the Heritage Square apartment complex, Danny heard a rattling noise on the window. It was Dele, making hand signals for Danny to open the door. Danny was glad to see him. He had not changed a bit, except for putting on a few pounds. That was expected, thought Danny as he remembered the McDonald's burger he'd eaten on the train. A quick hug followed.

"Welcome ma," said Dele to Evelyn as he slightly prostrated.

"How are you Dele? Wow, you are grown. Look, you have a mustache."

Dele blushed and took two bags from Chubi, while Danny followed suit and entered the apartment.

Danny woke up the next day to the aroma of fried eggs and sausage, coming from the kitchen. He barely had the energy to keep his eyes open. Dele had gone to school. He was a sophomore at the University of District of Columbia and was majoring in Pre-Med. He would be going to work later for the afternoon shift at the Kentucky Fried Chicken restaurant in the north east section of D.C. They had been up late into the night, reminiscing about old times at the high school they'd both attended. Dele wanted all the gossip on his former classmates back in Nigeria. He had lost contact with most of them.

It was ten o'clock when Danny walked into the dinning room for breakfast. Evelyn had been knocking on his bedroom door, asking him to get dressed and come out and say hi to Bunmi. Danny was meeting her for the first time.

"This is Chubi's wife," said Evelyn. "She's had been working a double shift at Howard University Hospital in D.C."

She was tall, feisty and a bit slender, thought Danny. Not what he'd expected, especially after meeting Chubi.

"How are you? I hope you like the breakfast I made for you. Would you like some tea, orange juice or coffee?"

"Tea. Thank you."

As Danny munched on his last piece of toast, he could hear Chubi's voice from the living room. It sounded like he was having a serious discussion with a stranger. Danny leaned towards the door to hear their conversation.

"This could work," said the stranger. "The guy assured me at the Liberian consulate that the papers provided can be verified and are authentic."

"Very well, said Chubi. I told Chief Ladi and the General I would take care of Danny, but I can't discuss the details with his mum. She would freak out."

"What about the kid? Does he have the balls to follow through"?

"Chief Ladi gave me a heads-up about the kid's escapades back home in Nigeria. I can assure you, he's not a saint."

"Well, it's their money. Just make sure I get the two grand as discussed."

"I told you. I've got this."

Danny heard someone walking towards the door. He sat down abruptly and took a gulp of tea. It tasted nasty and cold.

It had been four days since Chubi had called Danny aside to inform him of his plans. He had started the conversation by asking about Danny's plans for after his mum returned to Nigeria. Chubi looked innocent as he spoke, and Danny went along with it.

"I don't know. I will have to get a job as soon as possible".

"How are you going to achieve that? I understand your parents hope you get permanent residency in the long-term.

However, they are ignorant of the U.S. immigration laws. You are in the U.S. on a visit visa which expires in a few weeks."

"Like I said, I don't know. Going back to Nigeria is not an option. Can you help me"? asked Danny.

"Sure. I don't want you to become an undocumented immigrant. I have a friend who can get you papers that classify you as a Liberian citizen."

"Liberian?" asked Danny.

Danny had done his research after eaves dropping on Chubi's conversation. It seemed the United States was the former colonial master of Liberia. They were currently granting Liberians who had fled the civil war refugee asylum status. Danny knew the whole history. The conflict had erupted after Charles Taylor led a coup d'état toppling a democratic elected government in the eighties. That was followed by growing discontent among some of the government officials, who created another rebel group.

"Yes. It's the only way I can think of to help you get legal residency," said Chubi. "Can you handle it?"

"Do I have a choice?"

"Don't tell your mum."

"Sure, you can count on me. Trust me, I don't want to get my mum worried either. When do we start?"

"I'm making the call right now. The whole set up should be ready by next week," said Chubi.

"Alright. Thanks a bunch sir."

Danny walked into his room, lay on his bed and put a pillow over his head. He wondered why his parents had not studied in the U.S years ago just as Chief Ladi had. That would have provided him a U.S. citizenship by birth just as Dele. Now he pondered the direction in which life was about to take him.

Chapter 7

THE ALARM CLOCK RANG AT 6:00 A.M. Danny turned it off. He was tired. He had not slept all night. He had an appointment with the United States Citizenship and Immigration Services at 8:00 a.m. He was a nervous wreck.

If he got caught, how will he explain this to his mum? What kind of questions were they going to ask?

"I can't back down now," he thought. Chubi had forfeited two grand to secure the documents needed for this interview today. Danny turned off his thoughts and went straight into the shower.

There was a knock at the bedroom door.

"Good morning" said Bunmi. "Breakfast is on the table."

"Good morning. Thank you. I'll be there in a few minutes."

Danny had to catch the orange line at New Carrolton Station to the USCIS office in Alexandria, Virginia. Chubi was waiting in the car outside to drop him off. Danny came out of the room, walked over to Evelyn and kissed her on the cheek.

"Good morning mum. I've got to go out with Chubi for a job opportunity. See you later."

"What about the breakfast Bunmi made for you?"

"Got to run mum. Tell her I'll eat it later."

"Alright dear. Good luck."

Danny hated lying to her. At least he was being honest about the food. He had totally lost his appetite.

He dashed out the door quickly.

Danny met the stranger who had made the arrangements for the documents as he exited the metro station.

"Hey, you look like you've seen a ghost. You've got to ease up man. Lighten up or you just might end up in jail and be deported back home. Here are your documents," he said. "Your birth cert stating you were born in Monrovia. Your date of birth remains the same, so to avoid you getting confused. That will be awkward, if you don't know your own date of birth. Alright, I've got to go. Good luck."

Before Danny could ask his name, he walked into the station and disappeared into the crowd.

Danny arrived at the USCIS office at 8:45. The building was heavily fortified, with armed guards in front of the security check point and metal detectors. After Danny was patted down, he got a ticket and was asked to sit in the waiting area with other applicants. Most were there from war torn countries and conflict zones. Some were with their entire family. He had ticket number ninety-two, and the last number called had been number forty-five.

It's going to be a long day, thought Danny.

He took a seat next to a Mexican family. Danny wanted to strike up a conversation just to kill time, but he knew to keep quiet. He needed to stay in line with the script he had researched for possible answers to the immigration agent's questions.

A couple of times, people were escorted in handcuffs from the interview room. Danny felt his heart racing fast. He began to sweat down his back, even though it was freezing outside. Almost everyone in the waiting room still had their jackets on.

"Calm down Danny. Calm down", he whispered under his breath.

Two hours later, number ninety-two flashed on the screen. He walked towards the interview room as if he were a pirate walking the plank. A blonde, blue-eyed, scrawny agent sat behind the desk. He looked as if he had not slept in days. His aura gave the impression that he was counting the days to retirement and a pension from uncle Sam.

"Good morning. I'm Special Agent Scott Walker. Please close the door and have a seat."

"Thank you", said Danny.

As he tried to close the door, he saw the handle was missing. He remembered the people he had seen being escorted out in handcuffs earlier. The interview room was a trap. Without a doubt, Agent Walker must have had the pleasure of making lots of arrest.

"I see you've applied for asylum and your birth certificate states you were born in Monrovia. I've been doing this job for a long time Mr. Adeyinka."

"Please just call me Danny."

"Okay Danny, I'm going to be straight with you. I think you are Nigerian. Though all your paperwork is complete and looks authentic, my gut feeling tells me you are Nigerian."

"I'm not Nigerian," said Danny.

"Tell me, how did you get to the shores of the U.S.?"

Danny was glad when he heard the question. It had been one of the questions he figured they would ask.

"During the war, I escaped to Yamoussoukro in Côte D'ivoire. That was where I boarded a plane to Canada and a few days later, crossed the border into Buffalo, New York."

"Really? So, what's the color of the uniform for the Canadian immigration officers?"

"White and navy blue," said Danny swiftly.

Agent Walker was quiet for a minute. "This is exactly why I believe you are Nigerian. You are too smart and cunning."

Danny wasn't sure whether that was an insult or compliment. The door opened and two more agents walked in.

"Can you stand up and place your hands on the wall, sir?" asked one of them.

Danny did as they asked. They patted him down from his collar to his shoes and checked his wallet. He felt relief when he remembered he'd removed everything except a five-dollar bill before leaving the apartment in the morning.

"Nothing here, sir," the agents said to Walker.

"Thank you gentlemen," he replied looking very disappointed.

When had Agent Walker called for back-up? He had been right in front of him the entire time. Maybe Walker had a secret button under his table. After the agents left the interview room, Walker apologized.

"I was just doing my job, he said. I'm still going to go with my gut feeling and deny your asylum application. Do you have anything else to tell me? Can you show me further evidence to corroborate your story?

"I can check when I get back home."

"Alright, your file will be on my desk. You are free to go. Here is my card, just in case you need to call me."

Danny said, "thank you" and quickly walked out of the building.

"That was close", he muttered.

Before he got back on the train, he threw Agent Walker's card in the bin. He hoped never to see that building again.

Chapter 8

IT HAD BEEN SIX YEARS SINCE EVELYN LEFT DANNY IN THE U.S. Danny became an undocumented immigrant once his B2 visa expired. Getting a job was challenging. Danny wandered for miles and filled out several job applications, but was unsuccessful. It wasn't long before Danny knew all the characters on the popular daytime soaps. After agonizing months of joblessness, he became frustrated. It had not been comfortable living with Chubi and Bunmi. Chubi came home from work drunk every day and slept on the couch snoring violently.

Who could blame him? thought Danny.

He had caught his wife cheating with Musa, an old friend of Chubi who also lived in the same apartment complex. Chubi began paying daily visits to the liquor store after his shift. The atmosphere was tense, and it was soon clear to Danny that he was no longer receiving free board. One day, Danny came home after a fruitless job hunt and decided to get something to eat. He was looking forward to the delicious leftovers from the day before. He opened the fridge and was greeted with a sign on the pot of egusi soup that read, "PLEASE DO NOT TOUCH." Danny called Dele over.

"Do you know anything about this?"

"Now you know why I eat at work before coming home. I don't need this crap," he said.

"Well, I don't have that luxury since I don't have a job yet. Until then, I'm just going to skim off the top."

"What if you get caught? asked Dele"

"Bite me," he replied.

Danny finally got his first job as a cook at Pizza Hut. Desperate, he had called Jimmy, his cousin living in Dallas for help. Jimmy's friend was a manager at the restaurant in the upper east side of Maryland. In six months after a lot of hard work, Danny became a Shift Manager and was proud of his achievement. He loved going to work. It was exciting. There was always some kind of drama at the restaurant with a customer. Once, a customer complained that her pizza did not look exactly like the one advertised on television. She created such a scene, the police were called to address the public disturbance.

Danny later got a job as a security guard and finally decided to start his own business, selling used cars. He was passionate about cars. He got the idea from Nnamdi, a regular at the bank where Danny worked. His company had won the contract after the bank got robbed during the previous Christmas.

Nnamdi came into the bank daily to make deposits. Danny admired the way he dressed and the cars he drove. Every time he came to the bank, he drove a different car. Danny got curious and approached him after his daily deposit.

"Good morning to you Danny. How are you today?"

"Great I suppose. Sorry to bother, are you a car dealer?"

"Yes, I am. Why do you ask?"

"Well, just wondering how I can get in on the action?"

"Oh! No worries. I go to different auto auctions every day to buy cars. Anytime you are free, you can join me."

"How about next Monday? I'll take the day off.

"Okay. Send me your address and I'll pick you up on Monday."

"Great," said Danny. He was excited.

At his first auction, Danny purchased two cars for five hundred dollars each, and sold them for a profit over the weekend. Danny had found his niche. He continued to gain notoriety and expanded the assets of his dealership. Ultimate Motors Inc. was established. Danny quit his security gig to pursue his business full-time.

Danny had lots of friends and developed a massive business network. He also attempted to further his education. He attended the University of District of Columbia but flunked most of his courses. He majored in Accounting and hated going to class. But Danny's popularity continued to grow. He frequented night clubs in the D.C. metro area. He partied hard every other weekend and accumulated a lengthy list of girlfriends from all walks of life.

It was customary for Danny to showcase his latest merchandise upon a grand entry at the clubs. He had exotic sport cars and SUVs. He always reserved a VIP spot right at the front door to guarantee a spectacular entrance. For Danny it was all about the publicity stunt. He secured a VIP lounge for his friends and potential dates and spent his nights sipping his favorite, Moët.

Over the years, Danny had gotten involved with the underworld. He wanted to turn more profits. Danny invested in cars known to the Nigerian syndicates as "Abiku". The term referred to the resurrection of an older sibling who had died, through the birth of another child to the same family or parents. Cars sold at Ultimate Motors, came from the streets of Baltimore and all over the northeast. The operation was carried out by the "B-More Boys," a notorious outfit that specialized in car theft and chop shops. The cars were given new VINs and titles and sold to Ultimate Motors for a fraction of the current retail value. Danny made the trip to New York via Baltimore at least twice a month with a couple of hired hands to drive the cars back to his lot in Laurel, Maryland. He had to make another run in couple of days. He got a call in the middle of the night about the arrivals of a new batch.

It was eight o'clock in the morning and Danny was fatigued from his trip to New York. He always drove the speed limit and was constantly on the lookout for police cruisers. It was tedious for him.

Danny knocked on Dexter's bedroom door. He knew Dexter had worked the late-night shift. Evelyn had brought Dexter to the U.S. two years after Danny's arrival. By this time, Danny and Dele had moved into their own apartments. They all parted amicably. Chubi needed his space as he pursued divorce proceedings from Bunmi. The divorce was brutal on the kids and was later finalized based on irreconcilable differences. Despite all his personal woes, Dele and Danny were grateful to him for providing a roof over their heads.

"Good morning, little brother".

"Good morning," he muttered under his breath, still half-asleep.

"Are you going to work today?"

"Nope. Why?"

"I'm going to downtown D.C to register the cars I bought at the auction in New York."

He was lying. Danny often made the trip with one of his staff, but it was a busy day at the lot. Nobody was available, and there were customers already waiting for the new shipment. He had always made it a priority not to involve family in his dealings with the underworld. He believed, that whatever the consequences, it was for him alone to bear. He made an exception.

"Sure, why not? I don't have any plans for the day. I need a break anyway."

"Great. Get in the shower and meet me in the living room in thirty minutes. I've got a lot to do today."

Two hours later, Danny and Dexter walked out of the Metro Station next to the DMV. The line was long, which was rare for a week day.

"This is something you'd expect on a Saturday, when everybody has the time to renew their tags or driver's license. Let's join the queue," said Danny.

After thirty minutes on the queue, Dexter jabbed Danny. He was distracted, trying to get the phone number of the lady standing in the next line.

"We're next."

"Alright man," he said irritated.

"Next!" shouted the DMV official.

"Good morning, I need new tags for couple of cars. Here are the titles and bills of sale."

She looked at the titles for a few seconds. Danny was getting nervous. He needed to think of a distraction.

"Do I know you from somewhere?" he said, smiling. Your face is familiar, because I don't forget beautiful faces."

She ignored him.

"Hold on a minute". She took the titles with her into a backroom. Danny felt they'd been waiting for over an hour, even though it had only been five minutes. Sweat trickled down his chest. He remembered the USCIS building in Virginia. He needed a drink.

Chapter 9

DANNY COULD SENSE SOMETHING WAS WRONG. It had been more than fifteen minutes. Should he walk away or stay put? To walk away would be admit that the documents were fakes. He had to trust his source. They had never let him down.

"I wonder what's taking so long," said Dexter.

"Don't know. Maybe the system is slow to verify the authenticity. It's a normal practice here at the DMV."

He was trying to stay calm and not make Dexter nervous. Finally, the woman came out of the backroom.

"I apologize for the delay. Our systems were a little bit slow and I had to get the approval from my boss. Everything is in order. Here are your registration papers and the tags for the cars. Thank you."

"Thank you," said Danny. He grabbed the papers and headed towards the exit.

Danny hoped the next train was on schedule. He and Dexter walked down the escalator to the lower deck, and suddenly Danny heard the words he dreaded most.

"FBI", "Freeze". All Danny could see was the end of the 9mm Glocks pointed towards them.

"Danny and Dexter Adeyinka, you are under arrest for forgery and document fraud. Put your hands above your head and take two steps backwards," said the lead agent. He was at least seven feet tall and approximately two hundred and fifty pounds.

Danny felt the cold steel handcuffs around his wrist and heard the agent on his walkie-talkie.

"Do you have the cars?"

"Negative. I repeat, negative. There are no cars out here matching the description on the titles."

"Ten-four," said the arresting agent. He and his colleagues walked Danny and Dexter back to the DMV.

They ushered them into the service elevator and up to the fourth floor. When the elevator door opened, Danny saw the "Federal Bureau of Investigation" sign on the wall.

Danny was surprised. He had been coming to the DMV for years, but had never known there was an FBI office in the same building. Danny muttered to Dexter not to say anything. The agents led them into different interrogation rooms. Danny was really concerned for Dexter.

Poor kid. What a day to get caught. How will I explain this to mum and dad?", he wondered.

A gray-haired man with a thick moustache walked into the interview room. He looked irritated at Danny's presence.

"I'm agent Donovan from the D.C FBI office. Did you understand your rights as they were read to you?

"Yes."

"Would you like to talk to me?"

"Of course not. I need a lawyer."

"Sure. However, you still must talk to us at some point. We have a great deal of evidence against you. We finally caught the Adeyinkas," he said with a smirk.

"Just to let you know, we are currently running your names through the USCIS database for an immigration detainer. Get comfortable, you're going to be here for a while. I can assure you, we are going to deport you guys back to Nigeria."

Danny did not hear what agent Donovan was saying. All he could think about was what could be happening with Dexter. Hopefully he wasn't having a breakdown.

After three hours of interrogation, Danny was taken to the basement for processing. Dexter was already there. He was glad to see him again, even though they were still in handcuffs.

"Adeyinka, Adeyinka" yelled the correctional officer at the D.C detention center. "You are required to stand before the magistrate for bond hearing."

Danny looked at his watch. It was four o'clock. He had been expecting the immigration officers to pick them up for deportation proceedings. Their names and fingerprints had been put in the system. It was just a matter of time before they found an immigration detainer. Obviously, something was amiss.

Danny wasn't complaining. He jumped up and grabbed Dexter. The correctional officer marched them in front of a TV screen, built into the wall. There were other inmates present. Some were there on drug charges, felony and misdemeanor charges. The room was filled. The magistrate appeared on the screen and the clerk called each case.

"Case number N51073. The United States versus Danny Adeyinka and Dexter Adeyinka. Forgery and Theft."

"This is not a trial, but a bond hearing. Do you understand?" asked the magistrate.

"Yes, we do."

"Your honor, though this is a first offence and a misdemeanor, we believe they are both a flight risk, since we cannot determine their country of origin," said the prosecutor.

"Do you have an immigration detainer for them?"

"No, your honor. Immigration has no record of such."

"Well, Mr Vitelli, that's for you and the arresting agents to figure out. I have a case load today and my job is to set their court dates. If at a later date, there are any developments, please let the court know."

"Yes, your honor."

"Your court date is scheduled for September 18. Based on the fact that this is your first offense, I will be releasing you both on your personal recognizance."

"Thank you, sir."

"Just make sure, you show up for your court date. If not, a bench warrant will be issued for your arrest. Good luck to you both. Next case!"

Danny and Dexter were released. As they walked out of the courthouse, Danny heard Donovan and another agent in a tense discussion.

"How come the USCIS did not have a detainer for them?" said agent Donovan.

"I don't know. They checked twice and still came up short."

"I know they are Nigerians and are in the U.S. illegally. I'm going to find out one way or the other."

Danny and Dexter hastened to the metro station. They couldn't afford to miss the next train.

Chapter 10

DANNY HAD SEEN A SIMILAR SCENE JUST TWO DAYS AGO on the Weather channel. A massive tornado had ripped through the town of Paris, Texas and it looked like a war zone. People's belongings were everywhere, and houses torn apart. That was the scene at home.

Apparently, the FBI with the aid of the Prince Georges County Police had issued a search warrant for their apartment. Neighbors told Danny it took place about 12 p.m. and all the streets in the neighborhood were cordoned off. The apartment was in total disarray. The sofas had been ripped to shreds, lamp-stands knocked over, air vents left open and their clothes all over the floor.

Dexter stood in the door way in silence and looking shocked beyond belief.

"Are you okay?" said Danny.

"I'm fine. I just don't believe what I'm looking at. What were they looking for Danny?"

"I don't know. They probably were wondering why an undocumented immigrant was registering so many cars."

"Is that a crime?" asked Dexter.

"No, but it looked suspicious. I only wished they had searched the house with care. Look at this place. Don't worry, I'll take care of it."

Danny knew exactly what they were looking for. He had been praying while they were locked up in the bull pen that the FBI would not find anything at his home. Danny had overheard one the agents on the walkie-talkie asking his colleagues whether they were at the residence already. Hopefully he had not been careless with documents, contact numbers and addresses of associates of the B-More Boys. If so, the FBI would be the least of his worries. Nevertheless, he did not want to cause Dexter to panic. Besides, that would mean admitting to everything, thereby making Dexter an accessory after the fact.

For now, he was glad. He knew the only reason the magistrate allowed them to be released was because the case had been dropped to a misdemeanor. If the FBI had found evidence of stolen cars and contacts with the B-More Boys in the New York area, they would have been charged with felonies.

He had been careful to make all his phone calls whenever he was at a girlfriend's place, and he had a lot of girlfriends. Danny had always been paranoid about someone bugging his phone or following him home. Whenever he came back from Baltimore or New York, he never went home directly. He stayed in a hotel for at least a week. Most of his transactions were in cash. However, he was more worried about being trailed by elements of the B-More Boys. Danny knew they wanted a leverage in case a deal went south. Like now, if he were ever busted by the FBI and was considering becoming an informant, the gang could kidnap family members, friends and associates as leverage. It was always a priority for Danny to stay one step ahead of both the B-More Boys and the FBI. So far, Danny had kept everyone at bay, but it was just a matter of time. He could feel it in his guts.

Danny was not sure why the courthouse was crowded. After the lawyer from the Office of the Public Defender introduced himself, Dexter found a seat for both of them at the end of the aisle close to the jury box. They had not said much to each other this morning. It was clear that Dexter was nervous. Danny could not afford to show any sign of fear, though he was really concerned. However, he felt comforted by the fact that the FBI had not found any evidence tying him to the stolen cars. He expected the case to be dismissed.

Next time, I will be more careful, he thought.

Just before he could finish his thought, the door to the judge's chamber opened and the bailiff yelled out.

"All rise! The Honorable Judge J.B Stanley presiding"

Everyone remained standing until the judge was seated.

Immediately the bailiff called the first case. Two men in black suits wearing black gloves stood opposite Danny and Dexter.

"Danny Adeyinka, please step out of the courtroom," said the man on the left side.

This has to be the FBI. Now what? thought Danny.

As he rose, the judge yelled across the courtroom.

"What's going on in my courtroom?"

The prosecutor approached the Judge. Danny could hear him whispering.

"Your honor, we are not trying to disrespect your courtroom. The U.S. Attorney for the Southern District of Maryland , John Rosenberg, has brought new charges against Mr. Danny Adeyinka on a superseding indictment. These agents are here to arrest him for arraignment before Judge Machete at the U.S. District Court, Greenbelt Division in Maryland."

"This is my courtroom. I will not allow such charade during court proceedings. Do you understand?"

"Yes, your honor. As a result of this new development, we ask for a dismissal of the case before this court regarding Mr. Danny and Dexter Adeyinka."

"So be it."

"Thank you, your honor."

The agents placed Danny in handcuffs.

"Danny Adeyinka, you are under arrest for False Loan Application. You have the right to remain silent. Anything you say can and will be used against you in a court of law. You have the right to an attorney. If you cannot afford an attorney, one will be provided for you. Do you understand the rights I have just read to you?"

The agents held Danny on each arm and walked him out of the courtroom, straight into the waiting elevator. An unmarked car was waiting, along with Agent Donovan and eight other agents.

"Hey Ramirez! This is my case. You are out of order," said Donovan.

"No were not. The U.S attorney signed off this case to the Secret Service since the crime committed constitutes financial fraud. That's exactly our jurisdiction. Now, stand down."

While the men in suits argued, Danny could not figure out who'd given him up.

"What loan?" he asked. I have never been careless with paper trails, he thought.

Finally, agent Ramirez got in the driver seat of the cruiser and screeched off. His colleague in the passenger seat glanced at him, gesturing at his watch.

"Don't worry, I know its Friday," said Ramirez. "We're going to make it before Judge Machete leaves for the day. Trust me; the U.S Marshals will wait for this one. They have their instructions. I don't want to be stuck with paperwork over the weekend either. He is now the U.S. Marshal's problem, not ours."

They made their way through the traffic. Danny was grateful that Dexter was free and would not be in danger of deportation. As they got on the Baltimore-Washington Parkway, Danny lowered the window to enjoy the breeze. He didn't know when he would get the opportunity again.

Chapter 11

THE DRIVE TO LA PLATA WAS TEDIOUS. Danny sat by the door of the paddy wagon, which was transporting them to Charles County Detention Center after his arraignment before Judge Machete. The indictment by the grand jury had been based on the evidence against Jerry Jones, who'd been arrested two weeks earlier. The bank discovered the VIN on the chassis was different from the VIN on the title when Jerry defaulted on his loan and the car was repossessed. Danny had purchased the Acura Legend for Jerry from the B-More Boys as a favor. He was a family friend and had had some financial challenges after losing his job. Danny had refused his request a couple of times since he never mixed business with friends or family, but had decided to make an exception when Jerry's mother passed away suddenly.

The Feds had been looking for a way to arrest Danny after he had slipped through the crack during his last arrest in D.C. It had been a major embarrassment for the FBI and the USCIS after the fiasco at the courthouse. Agent Donovan had sworn to arrest Danny in the future, whatever the cost. To his delight, Agent Ramirez had informed him that Danny had finally admitted to being an undocumented immigrant from Nigeria during the arraignment and had been detained immediately. The evidence was undisputed and with the aid of Jerry as a witness for the Feds, Danny had no choice but to surrender.

It was 7 p.m. when Danny was placed in D-Pod after he was processed at the detention center. He was tired and hungry. All he'd eating was a crusty baloney sandwich with a tad of mustard and small cup of Pepsi at the courthouse before his arraignment. Just before assigning him his cell, a correctional officer came in with a food tray.

She was African-American, about five feet tall and in her thirties. She seemed a little bit unkempt. Her braids looked more than three months old, judging by the amount of hair growth along her hairline and between each braid. Though she was young and fit, she looked much older. Her nametag read Keisha Adekunle. Danny was curious about her origin, but was not in the mood for a conversation.

"Mr Adeyinka, today is your lucky day," she said. "Agent Ramirez called us ahead of your arrival to keep your dinner because they might be arriving late. Who are you?" she asked

"Nobody," Danny said.

All Danny wanted was to eat and get some sleep. It had been a long day. After a minute or two, Danny felt bad for having been so snappy at her. She probably was just trying to lighten me up, he thought.

"I'm sorry I snapped at you. Today has been crazy. Have you heard the saying when it rains, it pours?"

"Sure. We have lots of inmates coming through here every day, but you look really nervous and like you don't belong here."

Danny wondered, who belonged there if not him. His tray contained two Sloppy Joe sandwiches, an apple and a cup of orange drink that tasted like diluted Kool Aid. At this point, Danny knew he couldn't afford to be choosy. He started woofing down the food before somebody changed their mind.

As he took the last sip, another officer walked into the Pod and told officer Adekunle he would be taking over.

"This is officer Jenko. He will be assigning your cell tonight. Tomorrow you will be able to access the entire jail population and commissary. Good night."

"Good night" replied Danny.

Officer Jenko yanked his radio from his waist and yelled, "Open cell forty-five." Immediately, Danny heard the metal doors on the north side of the pod roll backwards. As they walked to the cell, faces behind those metal doors looked out with curiosity. Danny could feel the intense scrutiny by the rest of the inmates. He was being vetted.

A large figure lay on the lower mattress of the bunk in the cell. Officer Jenko handed Danny a few toiletries, a towel and a notepad. He pushed Danny into the cell and yelled into his radio "Lock up forty-five." The door slammed behind him and officer Jenko was out of sight.

"Hey man! What's up? Danny said in a deep tone."

He had put up a mean looking face to send a signal to his cell mate not to have any ideas regarding any form of aggression or sexual assault. Danny was terrified but could not afford to show any behavior that would be interpreted as a sign of weakness. He had heard lots of stories from his former colleagues and the movies did not make it easier either.

"Yeah man, what's up? They call me "Lil Mike". What's your name?"

"You can call me Danny."

As the man leaned forward for a handshake, Danny saw him clearly. Lil Mike was at least seven feet five inches tall. He looked like he was in his late twenties and weighed about three hundred pounds. Danny could hear him breathe as if it was a chore and an exercise. He was an intimidating figure and Danny wondered what his chances of surviving were if Lil Mike decided to pounce on him in the middle of the night.

"Where are you from?" asked Lil Mike.

"I'm from Nigeria."

"Nigeria? Oh man, oh man. I know lots of Nigerians from my neighborhood."

"Really? What neighborhood is that?"

"I'm from Baltimore.

"In fact, I'm here because a Nigerian snitched on me."

"Wow! Sorry about that, said Danny.

Now he was really concerned for his safety. Could this be a trap? The only person who had the motive and the means to pull such a move would be Agent Donovan. He knew Donovan still had a vendetta after the embarrassment to the FBI office in Washington D.C. However, the District Court of Maryland was not his jurisdiction and it was Agent Ramirez that had transported him to the detention center. He shrugged it off as a coincidence.

"What are you in for? Danny asked.

"Conspiracy to distribute and possession of narcotics. What about you?"

"False Loan Application."

"What the heck kind of charge is that?

"It's a white-collar crime."

"What's a white-collar crime?"

Danny was not in the mood to carry on the conversation. He didn't want any information used against him in trial, if his cellmate turned out to be an informant.

"It's a form of financial fraud. What time do they serve breakfast here?"

Danny needed to change the conversation without being rude. It was important to have a great rapport with Lil Mike if he was going to survive in this detention center.

"6 a.m."

"Thanks. I think I'm going to get some sleep. I'm beat."

Danny hopped on the upper mattress on the double bunk and made a false pretense of yawning loudly.

"I feel you man," said Lil Mike.

That was the last thing Danny heard until the cell doors for the entire pod opened at 6 a.m.

IT HAD BEEN A WEEK SINCE DANNY ARRIVED AT THE
DETENTION CENTER. So far, Lil Mike had been an asset. He
knew every player at the center who could get all sorts of contraband depending on the price. By the end of the weekend,
Danny knew almost everything about Lil Mike. He was very
talkative. He had been in that cell alone for about a year and
Danny guessed he was starved for attention.

Who knew hardened criminals could suffer from loneliness.

Lil Mike was a family man. He had the pictures of his baby
mama and his two daughters taped to the bottom of Danny's
bunk. He talked about them every night. Sometimes, Danny
wondered if Lil Mike could be on the brink of a breakdown. Behind that tough guy exterior, Danny could see fear and panic all
over his face, especially when his lawyer told him the Feds were
offering him a fifteen-year sentence in exchange for a plea deal.
It wasn't rocket science to see that he did not have much of a
choice. Its either that or life in prison. Lil Mike had been involved
in the drug business most of his life. He had never worked a le-
gitimate job and had dropped out of school. All he had was a
third grade education. Though he was from Baltimore originally,
Lil Mike grew up in southeast. A low-income and crime-infested
area. Danny was very familiar with that district. Every time he
received a new merchandise from the B-More Boys, he took the
cars to south-east to hook them up with accessories such as
chrome wheels, bass woofers, window tints, amplifiers and a
new paint job if necessary. Often, those accessories were provided at a great discount through his connections there. Danny
suspect they were stolen but knew better than to ask questions.

"Hey Danny."

"What's up Lil Mike?"

"I need a favor. I need you to help me write a letter to
Shantel."

"Again? Didn't we just write to her four days ago?"

"Yeah, but I haven't heard back. I tried to call her, but she won't accept my collect calls. Not sure what is going on. It's been three months since I heard from her and the kids."

"Calm down. I'm sure there is a good explanation for this."

Danny suspect Shantel might have moved on with her life. In every picture Lil Mike showed him, she was adorned in expensive jewelry, skimpy dresses, high heels, fur coats and weave-on. Danny had dated a lot of ladies like Shantel in the south-east district and they all seemed to graduate from the same school of thought. They had serious needs. If you were not available to pay the bills, there was always someone else to replace you.

Danny had to think of his safety. Though Lil Mike has been a good cell mate so far, telling him the truth might change all that in a blink of an eye. A man facing fifteen years or a life sentence, could conclude he had nothing to lose and become a time bomb waiting to explode. He had to think fast.

"Did you contact her mum or any other family member?"

"Yeah. I spoke to her sister, but all I got was an attitude and a warning never to call their family home again. She never liked me anyways and the feeling is mutual."

"Okay. I'll write the letter for you after the 12 p.m. count."

As they started walking back to their cell, the siren sounded off in the distance.

Chapter 12

THE COUNT WAS OVER WITHIN AN HOUR. Danny hated standing by his bed, being counted like a farm animal. In the past, inmates had been found dead, placed on their beds and covered up to look like they were asleep. By now, Danny was used to it. At first it was an inconvenience, especially during the 12 p.m. count when most of the inmates were watching their favorite day time soaps. Danny preferred *The Young & The Restless*.

This week there was a rumor that Victor Newman's plane had crashed and disappeared over the Rockies. There was going to be a showdown between Jack and Victoria over who would be the next CEO of Newman Enterprises. Initially, Danny could not understand why the inmates took an interest in what he considered a "chick flick." Lil Mike had warned Danny not to ever change the channel when the soaps were on. Inmates had been shanked for that same reason. Lil Mike explained further that the soaps provided the inmates something to look forward to. For a few hours, they forgot their court cases and the lengthy sentences awaiting them. The detention center encouraged them to watch, to reduce the tension and the risk to its officers.

Danny had placed the letter he wrote to Shantel below Lil Mike's pillow while he snored. As he walked out of his cell, he saw officer Adekunle at the pod entrance.

"Danny Adeyinka," she yelled.

"Yeah, what's up?"

"You have a visitor. Get your jump suit."

"Sure. Give me five minutes."

Danny grabbed his jump suit from the bed and hurried downstairs to the pod exit.

"Turn around and place your hands behind you," she said with handcuffs in full view.

Who could it be? Dexter had told him he would be there on Saturday. It was Wednesday. They walked past the other pods towards the visitor's room on the west wing. Then officer Adekunle turned eastward and headed into a small room. Agent Ramirez and another suit sat next to him, grinning.

"Good day Danny," said Ramirez. Are they treating you well over here?"

"What do you care?"

"I'm not the enemy Danny. Don't hate."

"What do you want?"

"This is Assistant U.S. Attorney Edward Reese. He would like to have a few words with you."

Edward Reese had very thick eyebrows and a slick moustache. He reminded Danny of Sam Elliot in the movie *Tombstone*.

"Good day, Mr Adeyinka. You have been remanded without bail for the charge of False Loan Application. However, we uncovered some documents involving wire transfers and fraudulent checks into a dummy account registered under the name "Giorgio Ligotti" to the tune of a hundred thousand dollars with a Bank One outfit in Dallas Texas during the investigation of your friend Jerry. As a result, the grand jury has indicted you for Bank Fraud at the United States District Court, Northern District of Texas, Fort Worth Division. After your trial here in Maryland, you will be extradited to Texas to answer to the charges I just brought to your attention. Do you understand all that has been said so far?"

Danny sat speechless. He was hoping they were here to tell him that the charges had been dropped or at least reduced to a misdemeanor.

Ramirez leaned forward and raised his right hand in the air.

"What Mr. Reese is trying to say is that, if you cooperate with us, we can work something out by reducing your sentence to "time served" and put off your deportation order from the USCIS."

"Really? In exchange for what?", Danny asked.

"We know that the B-More Boys have expanded their operations into the DC metro area. They were your business partners and we were wondering if you will be willing to help us gain access to the inner workings of the group."

"Are you nuts, Ramirez? If you are, I can assure you I'm not."

"This is a good deal Danny. With this new development, you are going to be sentenced to ten years or more."

"For you or for me? Do you understand that some of those guys are Nigerians? What about my family?"

"What about them?" said Ramirez.

"Who is going to protect them back home? Your jurisdiction is confined to the United States. I don't give a hoot how good your offer is, I'm not doing it. I'll do my time and hopefully come out alive and not end up in a body bag."

"Alright, if you ever change your mind, here is my card. All my numbers are there, you can reach me anytime."

"Danny stood up and banged on the door. Officer Adekunle opened the door with her handcuffs in plain sight."

"Ready to go back to your pod?"

"Yes please."

LIL MIKE WAS CONCERNED FOR DANNY. It had been two days since the visit from the Secret Service and he had refused to come out of the cell. All attempts to get his mind off the development were futile. He lay staring at the ceiling for hours. He had told the General and his mum that he had been arrested for being an undocumented immigrant and that he would be released very soon.

"How am I going to explain myself now?" he muttered.

"There is no way to minimize this any further. My life is over as I know it."

According to Dexter, there was a rumor spreading within the Nigerian community in Maryland that Danny had been arrested on a ship loaded with two hundred shipping containers filled with exotic cars at the Baltimore harbor and would most likely be sentenced to life. Danny feared Dele and Chubi might have contacted his parents and told them the rumors.

Lil Mike had not been sleeping well either. He could hear Danny crying in the middle of the night and muttering words he could not understand. Lil Mike brought Danny's lunch to the cell, but he barely touched it. It was now 5 p.m. and most of the inmates were heading to the courtyard.

"Hey Danny, I'm going to the gym. You wanna come?"

"No thanks," he muttered.

"You know, staying indoors all day is not going to make your problems go away. Why don't you come with me? It might take a load off. Look on the bright side, I know how you feel. I'm facing the same situation."

"Thanks man, but I'll stay right here."

"Okay, have it your way."

Danny had told Lil Mike about the new charges from Dallas Texas, but purposely left out the offer to become an informant. Inmates don't take too kindly to snitches. Danny worried about what Ramirez had said regarding the B-More Boys expansion into the DC metro. The detention center had a substantial amount of their gang members awaiting trial, including in his Pod.

Who knows if Lil Mike was one of them. I can't trust anybody if I'm going to survive and stay alive, he thought.

Danny heard a knock on his cell door. It was Jim Garret from cell twenty-five. A middle-aged man with massive dreadlocks and a native of Jamaica. He'd grown up on the east side of Baltimore. He had already been sentenced to life on a drug and murder charge and was into the tenth year on his sentence. Danny had always wondered what was wrong with him. He walked around all day with a smile on his face, trying to make friends with everyone in the pod. Danny had assumed he was fishing for anyone with a burden of guilt, ready to confess, thereby becoming an informant and candidate for a reduced sentence. He was brought to the detention center from the Federal Correctional Institute at Allenwood, Pennsylvania where he was serving his time because had to appear in court for his appeal. Danny made every effort to avoid him.

"Hey Danny, can I have a word with you?"

Danny was terrified. Lil Mike had gone to the recreation area, with the pod basically empty.

Danny got up from his bunk, put up a bold face and stepped outside into the hallway.

"We heard of your predicament and how the Feds are trying to railroad you."

"We?" said Danny.

"Yes. The Christian Brotherhood. We would like to invite you to for Bible Study."

"Sorry, I don't understand. Why am I being invited?"

"We meet at 8 p.m. in cell twenty on Wednesdays and Fridays. Will you come?"

"Not sure, but thanks for the invite anyway."

"You're welcome," he said as he walked away, still smiling."

What did he have to lose? He would hear what they had to say. At this point, he needed all the help he could get.

Chapter 13

DANNY GREW UP IN THE CHURCH, BUT LOST IN-
TEREST AS A TEENAGER. He felt the church had
nothing to offer him. After the General became a born-
again Christian, he joined the Mountain Point church in Lagos.
They frowned upon women wearing jewelry and pants. When
the General Overseer was not around, a tape of his sermon
blasted through the auditorium speakers. Ushers used whips to
wake those who dared to nap. The church operated just shy of
the same method applied by the detention center and its officers.
It felt more like an indoctrination.

Evelyn disliked the church's doctrine. She preferred to wor-
ship at the liberal and charismatic Life Church. Danny loved at-
tending with Evelyn whenever he escaped from the clutches of
the General. The girls at this church were much prettier. Going
to Bible study and being around a bunch of Christians was not
intimidating. It's a world he understood well, though he
couldn't remember the last time he prayed.

Danny joined the group at 8:30 p.m. He needed to give the
impression that his appearance was for their benefit and not his.
The room was full. Danny knew most of the men there from card
games in the common room. Jim was sitting at the head of the
lower bunk holding a Bible. He motioned for Danny to sit next
to him. They had been singing the line, "Trust and obey, for
there is no other way to be happy in Jesus."

After the opening prayer, Jim stood in front of the group.

"Today, we have a guest in our midst. Please welcome
Danny. He is joining us for the first time. We hope you will find

peace as you walk through the journey of life."

Danny felt a little bit embarrassed, but everyone was friendly. People shared their testimonies of overcoming the challenges of being separated from family members despite their long sentences. Some were there fighting deportation orders, after having lived in the United States since kindergarten. Most of them were caught off guard by the subtle change of the "Illegal Immigration Reform Act" of 1996 signed by President Bill Clinton. Previously, deportation was only possible with sentences of five years or more, but under the new law, shoplifting would get you deported.

At the end, prayers were offered for those who requested for it. Most of the prayers were geared towards God's favor for those heading to court for sentencing. Danny understood what that felt like. He was in the same boat. His fate was in the hands of someone else. As he walked back to his cell, Jim caught up with him.

"Did you enjoy the Bible study?" Jim asked.

"I did enjoy the company of the other inmates. It made me feel that I was not alone. However, I don't think God can solve my problems right now."

"Why would you say that?"

"Look, I appreciate you looking out for me, but this is real life. I've committed so many atrocities and hurt many people, especially those close to me. Why would God forgive me? I can't even forgive myself. I think it was mistake coming here today."

Jim started laughing hysterically.

"What's so funny?" asked Danny irritated.

"Nothing bro. You just reminded me of me. I was just like you when I got arrested years ago. I was in a dark place. I felt my life was over. I was sentenced to life in prison and I thought I was better off dead. I was angry and bitter. But God saved me bro. I surrendered my life and accepted Christ as my lord and savior. Today, people see me smiling every day and think I'm insane. I'm sure you've had the same thought."

"No, I haven't," lied Danny.

"Well, what does it matter? God has given me a fresh start in life and my joy knows no bounds."

"Fresh start? Haven't you been incarcerated for over ten years now? At least so I heard," he said in a hush tone.

"Don't worry, everyone knows. Yes, it is a fresh start for me. The Bible tells us in the book of second Corinthians, chapter five and verse seventeen, 'Anyone who belongs to Christ has become a new person. The old life is gone; a new life has begun.' At first, it did not make sense to me either, until I understood that if Christ died and forgave my sins, I had to let go of the past and forgive myself also. Since then, I've had peace that surpasses even my understanding and that was the beginning of my journey."

"Wow! That's a lot to take in."

Suddenly, the words "lights out in fifteen minutes" blurted through the pod's intercom.

"Think about it," said Jim. There are worse things that could happen to a man. Have a good night."

"Good night," Danny replied.

He walked into his cell. Lil Mike was on his bunk with a letter in his hands. Danny hoped it was good news, otherwise it was going to be long night. Five minutes later, the doors slammed shut.

IT WAS ALMOST TIME FOR THE 12 P.M. COUNT THE NEXT DAY WHEN DANNY WOKE UP. Lil Mike had finally gotten a reply from Shantel. As suspected, she had a new man in her life who was willing to take care of the children as his own. Furthermore, she would not be coming over to visit him at the center anytime soon. This was the first time Danny saw Lil Mike cry. Danny comforted him by reminding him nobody could replace him as a father to his kids

Officer Jenko stood at the door of the cell.

"Danny, you have a visitor."

"Who is it?"

Danny was not in the mood for another bout with agent Ramirez and his colleagues from the office of the U.S attorney.

"I believe it's your lawyer."

"Okay. I'll be down in five minutes."

Danny was glad for the visit but still wondered who it might be. On the day he was arraigned before Judge Machete, a lawyer from the Public Defender's Office had represented Danny just for that day since it was the end of the day on Friday before the court closed for the weekend. He was informed by the court that he would be appointed a lawyer before the next court date.

Danny shook his wrists after Officer Jenko took off the handcuffs. He'd had it on too tight. Other inmates complained about the same thing. Just before coming out of his cell, he'd rubbed Vaseline around his wrists. Seated at the table was a young white lady with scruffy blonde hair, blue eyes and beautiful eyebrows. Her suit looked expensive, nicely trimmed and fitted. If Danny didn't know better, she could have passed as a high school student visiting her dad at the center.

"Are you okay?" she said.

"Who are you?"

"My name is Susan Macarthy. I'm an attorney with Macarthy & Macarthy. The court appointed me to represent you. I just got your file yesterday, so I'm going to need your help to fill me in on anything you think I missed or omitted regarding your case."

"How old are you?" asked Danny.

"How is that related to your case? And by the way, it's none of your business."

"Well, look here missy. This is my life we are talking about. I need to know if you are experienced enough to be in the driver's seat. You are in the big-league, lady. So, forgive me if I question why the court has appointed me a fresh law school graduate."

"Mr Adeyinka! I'm the youngest junior partner at my firm, graduated from Harvard Law at the top of my class and was a member of the Student Law Review Forum. Mostly, I practice corporate law, but as lawyers, we are required to take on at least fifty hours of pro-bono cases per year. So, if you have a problem with me taking your case, I will be glad to inform the court at your next court date and you will be provided with an alternative. So, forgive me when I ask you to cut the crap and let me do my job. Either way, I'm on the clock. Like you said, it's your life we are talking about. What's it going be Mr Adeyinka?"

"Alright! You don't have to be that mean. Sure, you can represent me."

"Good. So, according to your file, you are being charged with False Loan Application from the U.S District Court in Greenbelt, Maryland. You are also being charged with Bank Fraud at the United States District Court, Northern District of Texas, Fort Worth Division; and you are currently being held without bond because there is an immigration detainer for deportation proceedings. Is that correct?"

"Correct."

"Mr Adeyinka."

"Please, call me Danny."

"Okay Danny. My philosophy is simple, with the aid of a simple question to arrive at a simple answer. It's based on the ability to assess the seriousness of your situation and determine the level of trust between my clients and I. Remember, all our conversation is protected under the attorney-client privilege.

"Did you do it?"

"Danny remembered the words of Jim Garret as he quoted the scripture from the Bible about anyone in Christ having a fresh start, their old life gone. Danny was not sure yet about being in Christ, but it would be nice to have a fresh start. He figured the only forward was to admit everything."

"Yes, I did it. Everything stated in that file is accurate."

"Okay, we are making progress. Here is the deal. I spoke to the assistant U.S Attorney today and they are offering you a plea deal. Time served and no deportation in exchange for information regarding the inner workings of the B-More Boys and to testify at trial."

"Just like I told agent Ramirez and Mr. Reese, I'm not suicidal and would not compromise the safety of my family back in Nigeria just to get out of prison early. This is non-negotiable. So, what's next?"

"My guess? They will try to railroad you by recommending to the judge, the maximum sentence according to Title 18 U.S. Code 1344. That's thirty years. They hope this will scare you to cooperate with them. I don't want you to worry about that. It's quite rare for judges to depart from the Federal sentencing guidelines, which limits their discretion. They are required to follow the pre-sentence report recommended and submitted by the U.S Probation Officer."

"What's your advice? asked Danny."

"Have you ever heard of Rule 20?"

"Nope, what is it?"

"Basically, it's the transfer of the prosecution from the district that issued the indictment and where a warrant is pending to the district where the inmate is in custody. This is based on the prerequisite that there is a plea deal and you will not be going to trial. The evidence against you is overwhelming and between you and I, you are not innocent of the charges against you. Hence, my plan is to confer with the Assistant U.S Attorney - Edward Reese, and convince him that you will accept a new plea deal without any condition attached for both charges, have the case transferred from Texas to Maryland to avoid extradition, saving the court time and money. This way, we can ask the court to sentence you concurrently on both charges."

"Is there a risk?"

"Yes".

"Okay, let's have it."

"Well…even if I can convince Edward Reese and his colleague in Texas, the judge is not under any obligation to accept a plea deal agreement between you and the DA's office. Nor is the judge obliged to accept the Rule 20. However, I'm optimistic. This is an election cycle and number of convictions matters."

"Do you know the judge appointed to my case?"

"It's Judge Machete. I believed he handled your arraignment. This will be my first appearance before him, and I heard his hardline reputation lives up to his name. Do you believe in God, Mr. Adeyinka?"

This has to be serious, thought Danny. She had used his last name.

"I don't know."

"Well, I'll suggest you figure it out quick, because it's time to pray for mercy and favor. Just as you said earlier, you are now in the big league."

"Touché", muttered Danny.

"Your next court date is on November 21. Good bye, Danny."

She left looking at her watch for the umpteenth time. Danny was tired from the information overload and could not believe he was looking forward to the serenity of his cell. Hopefully, Lil Mike was in a good mood and would crack some jokes tonight during lights out.

Chapter 14

THE BULL PEN BELOW THE COURTHOUSE WAS EX-CEPTIONALLY COLD as Danny waited for his case to be called before the judge. Susan was with Danny, informing him of a new plea deal by the prosecutor and prepping him on court etiquette. She made sure he had not come to court in his orange jump suit. Danny had on a gray sweat suit and pants he'd purchased from the center's commissary. Susan believed perception played a major role in most cases. As long as all the judges, prosecutors and members of the jury remained human, they were pre-disposed to a variety of biases. Though she was optimistic, Danny had his doubts.

Just last week, one of the inmates at D Pod had appealed his sentence before Judge Machete. Originally, his case had been before Judge Penny Sanders, a liberal judge with a central ideology. She had sentenced the inmate to four years imprisonment at the lower end of the sentencing guidelines for Illegal Reentry into the U.S. After Deportation, despite his prior convictions. Machete reviewed his case and amended his sentence to six years imprisonment, claiming that Judge Sanders had been too lenient and that the inmate did not deserve a downward review. That had sent shock waves throughout the detention center, especially for those whose cases were before Machete.

Danny was terrified and made sure he did not miss the next Bible study meetings at cell twenty. He had asked Jim Garret to pray for him regarding his court date, but Jim asked, "What is the point in praying to a God you don't believe in?"

Danny said, "I do believe in God, but I just don't think I'm ready to surrender my life to Christ just yet."

"God is not a slot machine brother. All you must do is believe in Him, confess your sins and repent of your ways. You can't have it both ways."

"Just like that, eh?"

"Yup! Just like that. Christ has already paid the price for you on the cross. I left a gift on your bed. It's a Bible. Read the gospel of John, chapter three, verse sixteen and Ephesians, chapter two, verse eight."

"Okay," said Danny.

"I'm still going to pray for your court date, however, remember what we discussed. God bless you."

Just then, a U.S Marshal banged on the door of the bullpen.

"Danny Adeyinka."

"Yes," yelled Danny.

"Be ready for court in five minutes."

"Okay."

Danny decided to get on his knees and pray.

"Lord, I'm not sure if you hear me. I have done a lot of awful things in the past. Please forgive me. I really need your help right now with this judge on my case. Grant me favor and let him be lenient on me. Have mercy on me, Lord. If you do this for me, I will serve you all the days of my life."

As he wiped the tears from his eyes, the marshal unlocked the door and Danny turned around with his hands behind him for the cuffs. It was time to face his fate.

THE COURTROOM WAS JUST AS COLD AS THE BULLPEN, BUT MUCH MORE INTIMIDATING. It was a large room with nicely polished oakwood benches on two isles of the room. Just before the benches are two large oakwood tables. One on each side of the courtroom for both the prosecution and defendant. Susan sat at the table for the defendant looking tired and defeated. She seemed worried and trying her best to put on a bold face. She motioned him to come over as the marshal took off the cuffs. As Danny approached Susan, he could see Dexter sitting in the second row and a couple of other people he suspected are from the media. Dexter looked overwhelmed and stressed. Poor kid! He has had to deal with creditors and what to do with all their belongings since they were evicted from their apartment for lack of payment. Danny felt sentenced already.

"Why did it take a while for the marshal to bring you up?" asked Susan.

"I was praying."

"Really?"

"Yeah."

"I hope God will hear you today, because we need all the help we can get. The U.S. Attorney is in the courtroom and the members of the media. I think we are going to be blindsided."

"All rise. The Honorable Judge R.U Machete presiding," called the bailiff.

Judge Machete walked in from his chambers and sat on the bench.

"Bailiff, call your case," he said.

"Case number 8:96-CR-02117-DKC. The United States versus Danny Adeyinka."

The judge motioned for the prosecution and the defense to approach the bench.

With one hand covering the microphone, Judge Machete whispered.

"Do I understand that the office of the U.S. Attorney has agreed to a plea deal on this case?"

"Yes, your honor," answered Mr. Reese.

"Great. Now, step back."

The judge leaned forward towards the microphone.

"Mr. Adeyinka, the prosecution has informed me of a plea deal between yourself and the office of the U.S. attorney. At this point, I would like to inform you that I am not bound by this agreement and personally I would prefer to see this case go to trial. You don't deserve the sentence recommended by this plea deal. However, I am in a good mood today and I guess you will be saving the tax-payers the cost of going through a trial. In that spirit, I will accept this deal."

"Thank you, your honor," Susan and Edward Reese replied.

"Mr. Adeyinka, were you under any duress or did anyone pressure you to agree to this plea bargain?"

"No, your honor."

"Do you have anything to say before I sentence you this morning?"

"Yes, your honor. I just want to apologize to all the victims that I hurt and the U.S government. I am sorry. I've asked God for forgiveness and I'm also asking for forgiveness and mercy today. I accept full responsibility for my actions. Thank you."

"You are hereby sentenced concurrently to three years in prison and five years' supervised release for the crime of Bank Fraud and False Loan Application. You will be housed at the medium-security prison at the Federal Correctional Institute, Petersburg Virginia. You are hereby ordered to pay a restitution of one hundred thousand dollars if not deported. Goodluck, Mr. Adeyinka."

"Thank you, your honor."

"All rise," said the bailiff.

The entire courtroom remained standing even after Machete had left for his chambers. Susan shook Danny's hand, beaming.

"Why are you smiling? Are you happy I got sentenced?"

"Are you kidding me? This a miracle. Do you realize what just happened here? You got three years concurrently instead of a minimum of ten years for each charge. This has never happened before in Judge Machete's courtroom. I didn't think he would go for it. If anything, I believe the U.S. Attorney only went along with the deal for political reasons to show the public that he is not all about the numbers, but also a man of compassion.

They knew Machete would never go for it. It would have been a win-win for them, but it backfired. Maybe, I need to go to church also."

"Maybe you should," Danny said smiling as the marshal placed him in handcuffs.

Dexter did not understand what had just happened. but Danny assured him he would explain it during his next visit at the detention center. Back at the bullpen, Danny got on his knees to give praise to God.

I guess, Jim was right all along. This feels like a fresh start, he thought.

He could not wait to tell Lil Mike what had happened. But then reconsidered. Maybe it wasn't such a good idea to tell Lil Mike. After all, the unprecedented sentence by Judge Machete could be misconstrued as a reward for becoming an informant. Danny was determined to get out of prison alive.

Chapter 15

THE RIDE TO PETERSBURG, VIRGINIA ON THE PRISON BUS was daunting and an experience Danny hoped not to repeat anytime soon. The day before, he'd been a bit emotional leaving Charles County Detention Center. Lil Mike had left the cell very early for morning chow to avoid saying goodbye. Danny understood. He would have done the same if the shoe was on the other foot. Danny and Lil Mike had become close friends, looking out for each other for the past few months. Though Lil Mike claimed he had gotten over Shantel, he often longed for the good old days and Danny wished he could move past that. Lately, his health has been deteriorating. Danny hoped to keep in touch, but knew better that he probably would not see his friend again.

The bus departed Charles County with just a few inmates, heading towards Baltimore. The U.S. Marshals decided to pick up other convicts designated for Petersburg from the Baltimore City Jail. This meant they would all have to sleep over and proceed in the morning. Compared to Charles County, Baltimore City Jail was a hell hole. The jail was overcrowded, drugs were sold in the presence of correction officers and inmates were in charge of allocating bed spaces to new inmates at a premium price. To Danny's amazement, inmates fraternized with correction officers in the pod. Danny and the other inmates in transit slept on plastic containers with their eyes open all night. Danny prayed for sunrise.

Danny was glad to see the U.S Marshals in the morning. He could not wait to be handcuffed and led to the bus. The bus arrived at F.C.I multiplex by 4 p.m. The institution sprawled across hundreds of hectares and was comprised of, Victorian Style buildings surrounded by layers of barbed wire and high security fences. The institution consisted of a Low-Security Prison, Medium Security Prison and a Camp for low flight risk offenders.

When it was Danny's turn to receive his prison allocation bag for toiletries, underwear and uniforms, the officer in charge of the laundry gazed at the paper he was holding.

"Are you Nigerian?" he asked.

"Yes."

"Someone wants to see you."

"Me? Sorry, I don't understand. I just got here."

"I know. Just follow me."

Danny was nervous. He had seen *Shawshank Redemption*. In the movie, Andy was ambushed and raped within the laundry facilities. Lil Mike had warned him how each prison abides by its own rules and unofficial policy. He advised Danny to blend in as much as possible and try not to make a fuss, so as not to attract too much attention from the guards and inmates. More importantly, the Christian Brotherhood had prayed over him for God's protection before departing the detention center.

As they walked through the laundry room, Danny started reciting the Book of Psalms, chapter twenty-three under his breath.

"The Lord is my shepherd, I shall not want. He makes me to lie down in green pastures."

Danny had been reading the Bible for the past couple of days. He had kept his promise of surrendering his life to Christ after Judge Machete's lenient sentence.

The officer suddenly stopped and looked backwards.

"Are you nervous? Don't worry, nothing bad is going to happen to you."

He opened the door and motioned for Danny to step inside.

The room was bright and musty. It had couple of shelves, lots of file cabinets, a table with office supplies and a chair. Standing by the table was a small black guy wearing an inmate allocated uniform with the name "Asha" and his inmate number taped to the front pocket of his shirt. He must have been at most five feet, five inches tall. His hair was neatly trimmed, his face clean shaven and his boots were finely polished. He wore thick glasses and was soft spoken.

"My name is Asha," he said, shaking Danny's hand. "You must be Danny. Hope the officer did not scare you?"

Danny knew the name "Asha" meant "eagle" in the Yoruba language. The eagle is revered in Africa for its stealth and swift approach when it hunts for prey. Danny hoped he was not classified as prey.

"A little bit, I must confess."

"Sorry about that. Welcome to Petersburg. As a Nigerian community, we try to lookout for one another. In here, there are all sorts of gangs and cliques you will need to watch out for."

"Like who?" replied Danny. He was curious.

"Well, there are four major gangs contending for control. The El-Rino gang and the B-More Boys control a significant portion of the prison, whilst the Gambino crime family and the Nation of Islam controls the rest. "

The mere thought of the B-More Boys sent shivers up Danny's spine. Agent Ramirez and Edward Reese had told him of their presence in the D.C. Metro area. This meant that, Danny might run into one them in this prison. Dexter had told him some of the B-More Boys had found him in Maryland after he got sentenced and threatened a reprisal if they ever found out Danny snitched on them.

"I thought this was supposed to be Club Fed. I heard there is a tennis court, movie theater and a state-of the-art library."

"It still is. It's sure better than the state prison. However, things can get ugly in the blink of an eye. If you mind your business here, you will be fine. The Nigerian community put together some commissary items you might need to hold you up till your commissary account is set up. Is that okay?"

"Sure. Thank you so much."

"Hey, no worries. I've made a special request for your room to be allocated in the hall where majority of us are housed. Like I said, we lookout for each other."

Danny thought of telling him about his worries concerning the B-More Boys but chose to stay silent. He had not snitched on anyone and there was probably nothing to worry about. Someone knocked and the door opened.

"Hey Asha, I've got to get him back to processing right now," said the correction officer.

"Okay. By the way, were you able to assign him to North Carolina Hall as I requested?"

"No. We don't have the bed space in North Carolina. Right now, he is designated for Lee Hall."

"Alright, thanks."

"You bet!"

"Danny, you don't have to worry. Though Lee Hall has some of the Nation of Islam and B-More Boys, we still have some friends over there. I will ask them to look out for you."

"Thanks, Asha."

Danny walked out. His life was in God's hand's now. Sometimes, being around too many Nigerians could be just as deadly. They could be nosy busy bodies who often snitched on each other. Danny knew a large contingent of Nigerians did business with the B-More Boys in New York. He figured his chances of survival might be best if blended in, instead of drawing attention to his nationality.

DANNY SETTLED INTO LEE HALL WITHOUT ANY IS-SUES. He had two new cell mates, Pookie from Baltimore and Deshawn from Washington D.C. They were both African-Americans and were not affiliated with any particular gang. Pookie was there on a gun possession conviction for five years, whilst Deshawn was already in his fourth year on a six-year sentence for a drug conviction. Notwithstanding, Pookie's body, especially his torso and arms told a different story, with at least four closed bullet and stab wounds. In Danny's attempt to get to know his cell mates better, he had asked Pookie about the bullet wounds.

"I was careless," he replied. He was not a talker like Lil Mike. Pookie spoke in short phrases and most of the time, he had his headphones on, listening to music on his iPod.

After the 4 p.m. count, Danny received a package from Dexter. It contained some books, magazines, legal documents and his old black address book. That address book held all the numbers and addresses of old girlfriends and female friends Danny had had some sort of relationship with. He guessed Dexter felt he might need to get in touch with friends on the outside. Danny wasn't sure what to do with the address book. As much as he appreciated the gesture, contacting these ladies could be a slippery slope, taking him to a place he knew too well, which would violate his promise to serve God.

Danny knew his demons. He'd never been platonic with most women. Danny was a sex addict. Sex had always been his mode of escape since the first encounter with a relative at the age of seven. Certainly, some of the women in the book probably wished him dead or at least neutered for his past sins. He had prayed to God earnestly to help him become faithful to just one woman, get married and settle down like a normal person when released. A few days later, he had a dream getting married to one of his ex-girlfriends. Nevertheless, Danny still felt the only solution was to burn his bridges with the past.

"Hey Pookie, do you have a permanent marker?" asked Danny.

"Nope. Ask Deshawn."

"Hey Deshawn, you got a permanent marker?"

"Yeah! I've got one. Just black though. What do you need it for, if you don't mind me asking?"

"I don't mind. Just trying to burn old bridges with my female friends from the past. That's all."

"What? Not me man. I'm holding on to everyone of them. You must have lost your mind."

"Probably, but I made my peace with God."

"Oh! I see…good for you. Let me know how that works out," he said with a smirk.

He crossed out every single one of them except for Lynn James. Every time he tried, he just couldn't do it. Pookie watched Danny tapping the marker and rattling the desk close to his bunk.

"Hey man! What's up?"

"Sorry Pookie. Just confused."

"About what?"

"I've got a name in my contact that I can't redact. Her name is Lynn. She is originally from South Carolina but spent most of her life in Maryland. I've known her for five years. She is great, very beautiful, well-mannered and never gives me any problems. Her parents are deacons at their church."

"Okay. So, what's the problem? I wish I had a girl in my life just like that."

"Well, it's been three years since we spoke after she kicked me out of her house. She said I can't just be showing up anytime I wanted and still not commit solely to her. All she ever wanted was to settle down and have a relationship with me and I wasn't having it at the time. I just couldn't quit as a player and a womanizer."

"Why don't you give her a call right now? You have nothing to lose, except your pride."

"I guess," said Danny.

Danny queued at the phone booths. There were only four phones on his floor for over sixty inmates. Just around six o'clock, it was his turn. He slowly dialed Lynn's number for a collect call. His tongue felt parched. The phone rang.

"This is a collect call from........"

"Danny Adeyinka," he said.

"An inmate from FCI Petersburg, Virginia. This call will be monitored. If you accept this call, please press one."

He heard a beep on the other end and her beautiful voice came through. She said hello.

Chapter 16

A FEW MINUTES BEFORE THE ALARM WENT OFF AT SEVEN, Danny jumped down from his bunk. It was visiting day and Lynn was coming to see him. It had been two weeks since Danny placed the call, and he was still a nervous wreck. At first, the conversation was a bit awkward, since he had not spoken to her for a while and had to explain why he was calling from a prison in Virginia. However, he had been reading the book of Hebrews in the Bible, which talked about "not casting away your confidence which has a great reward." With much courage, he explained to Lynn his past crimes and the sentence imposed on him by the court. He also explained his new-found faith in the Lord Jesus Christ and how he got saved. To Danny's surprise, she was not freaked out and was even glad to hear about his walk with God. Still, he expected to hear about her husband, three kids and the dog named Koko. He was sure she'd be living in a single-family home with a white picket fence. Instead, she said she was single and really missed him. Danny remembered the dream he'd had about getting married to one of his ex-girlfriends and broke down, tears rolling down his cheeks. After he hung up, he wiped his eyes and strutted back to his cell with a big smile and a grateful heart.

Visiting hours were from eight till four on weekends. Danny had his hair shaved, his prison-issued khakis starched and ironed, his boots shined to military standards. He needed to look his best for Lynn and waited patiently to hear his name called by the officer in charge of Lee Hall.

"Danny, you've got a visitor."

"Okay", replied Danny.

"Don't be nervous. It's going to be alright", said Pookie with a smile.

"Sure," he said, and gave a thumbs-up as he walked out towards the visitor's hall.

After Danny had been checked for contrabands by the correctional officers, he was ushered into the hall and there she was. Looking gorgeous as ever. She had on a simple white blouse and a nice green Capri pants that accentuated her curves. Her braids were nicely done, and her fingers and toes painted an exquisite glossy red. Danny walked up to her for the embrace and a kiss allowed by the prison.

Six hours went by fast. Danny and Lynn reminisced about old times and caught up with recent occurrences with family and friends. Though she had just lost both her parents within a three-year span, she was starting her own daycare center, which was flourishing and time consuming. Danny noticed two other individuals visiting another inmate, three rows down the hall, staring at him. They seemed familiar, but he couldn't place their faces. He tried to ignore their presence, but he had a nagging feeling they were members of the B-More Boys. He had probably engaged in some business dealings with them in the past. Lynn could tell he was distracted.

"Is everything okay?" she asked.

"Yeah. Just thought I saw some folks I recognized from the past sitting a few tables over."

"Who?"

"Don't look" Danny said. "It's probably nothing."

Danny did not want her to panic. The last thing Danny wanted was to allow his past to interrupt this beautiful day. However, she quickly reminded him that he wasn't talking to a stranger. She knew him better than anyone. She had known Danny for five years prior to their fallout and his disappearance. She could see he was nervous.

"Are you going to tell me what's really happening?" asked Lynn.

"Sorry. I don't want to bore you with my issues."

"Well, let me be the judge of that. I care for you, Danny, and I want to know whatever is going on with you."

Danny sighed heavily

"At the time of my arrest, the U.S. Attorney in Greenbelt tried to jam me up to make a deal to expose the gang I did business with, but I refused. The U.S Attorney was livid and didn't take the rejection well. As far as he was concerned, it was a political play to score points for the upcoming gubernatorial elections later this year. In a rebuttal move, they offered me another deal hoping the judge would deny the plea, forcing me into a trial that allowed for the statutory maximum sentence of thirty years. However, God favored me, and it backfired on them. I was sentenced to three years and five years supervised release if I don't get deported."

"Deported?" she asked alarmed.

"Yes, deported. There is an immigration detainer issued for me to be removed administratively upon my release."

"What does that mean?"

"It means the U.S government has a right to deport me without the due process of appearing before an immigration judge because I was never a legal resident of the United States."

Lynn's eyes got teary and Danny tried his best to re-assure her everything was going to be okay, even though he did not have a clue what the future held. He had not gone back to Nigeria since his departure seven years ago. Except what he heard from his parents and people who travelled back home, he knew very little about the status of Nigeria. Evelyn hadn't made it easier either. Every time he spoke to her, she always had a lot of sad stories about the hardship people were going through to make ends meet. He couldn't remember his mum ever saying anything positive about his country.

"Look at me Lynn," he said as she wiped her tears. "I still have about eighteen months left on my sentence and right now staying alive is my priority. We will cross that bridge when my release date gets closer."

"Okay," she said sounding upbeat. What about those guys checking you out over there?"

"Not sure, but I'm getting a feeling someone is spreading the news that I snitched on the B-More Boys to get such a reduced sentence."

"Doesn't that make it dangerous for you?"

"Yes, it does."

"Shouldn't we report this to somebody?"

"Right now, there's nothing to report and I don't want to make a case or rattle the cage if there is nothing to worry about."

"Okay. Promise me you will call me every night before my bedtime to let me know you are safe. This will be our code since your calls are monitored."

"Those collect calls are not cheap, dear. It's a complete rip-off. Everything here, including the commissary, is a monopoly. I heard Mrs Reagan, the former first lady has the contract to supply all the federal prisons in the country. Sometimes, whenever I hear a politician talking about getting tough on crime and legislating for a tougher crime prevention bill, it seems to equate to more dollar bills for the fat cats in Washington. This is modern day slavery. Where is CNN when you need them?"

The officer in charge announced five more minutes for all visits. Danny gave Lynn another hug and a kiss. Lynn tried not to cry, but it was an impossible feat. He watched her leave the hall with the other visitors and waved to her one last time before she disappeared beyond the exit door. Danny felt helpless and wished he could comfort her. Instead he was reminded that he was still in prison.

THE ALARM WENT OF AT 4 a.m. Danny had been assigned to work the morning shift in the kitchen, which meant going to bed early, a habit he'd never been accustomed to. Nevertheless, he was in a good mood. Spending some time with Lynn had taken his mind off the nagging feeling concerning the B-More Boys. They had spoken on the phone over the weekend and Danny was glad most of the conversation had been about the challenges she was facing with parents at the daycare center. A welcome distraction.

Danny reported to his supervisor, Officer Jimmy Ray Brown, a cowboy from Alabama. Everyone called him "Spits." Complimenting his government-issued uniform were, alligator-skin boots and a huge buckle belt around his huge tummy. He always had an empty transparent plastic bottle in his hands to catch his tobacco spittle. He barked out orders in a thick country accent to the inmates working. Danny tried to stay at least a good foot from him whenever he was barking those orders because of his bad breath.

Danny knocked on his door and heard "come in."

Are you the new guy assigned to me from Lee hall?

"Yes sir," replied Danny.

Now, look here boy. I don't care how you were assigned to my kitchen. What's important to me is your ability to carryout my orders. Right now, I'm fixing to leave for a meeting with the Warden and I'm assigning you to the "pick up crew."

"Pick-up?" asked Danny.

"Did I stutter? Yeah, the pick-up crew, boy. You and the rest of 'em' will be picking up crap after your fellow inmates during chow time. Are we clear?"

"Yes sir."

"Okay then. Why don't you grab an apron, a broom and make yourself useful."

Danny grabbed a broom and a dust pan behind the door and walked out fuming, in anger.

"Thank God for Jesus. Couple of years ago, I would have tied his moustache to the radiator just for fun," he muttered under his breath.

Danny swept up food debris as the inmates filed into the chow hall from their various dormitories. Inmates were released by halls depending on the results from the weekly inspections. The hall with the best report went to the chow hall first. This way, they got first choices of meals. Of course, the last hall got the scraps. This strategy was mostly appreciated by the inmates, especially when rice and baked chicken was on the menu. Nobody seemed to care if their hall was in last place if Sloppy Joes were being served.

However, Danny figured he'd gotten this job because of Asha. A perk for being Nigerian. Working in the kitchen gave Danny unfettered access to food and he had no complains there. Two hours into the breakfast period, North Carolina hall's turn to head for chow. Danny saw Asha on the queue and decided to sweep towards his direction. Someone bumped Danny, making him drop the broom and dust pan. It was the guy from the visitor's hall over the weekend.

"Watch where you are going" he said.

"Sorry about that bro. Didn't see you coming."

"You need to be sorry alright, just like your day is coming courtesy of the B-More Boys."

"What? Do I know you?" asked Danny.

Asha stepped between them.

"Is everything alright Brian?" asked Asha.

"It's all good. Ask your homeboy." as he walked away.

"What's going on Danny?"

"Not sure, Asha." Though he put up a brave face, he was a little shaken, scared and flustered.

"I was just on my way to see you. We need to talk."

"Okay. Meet me at the gym after the 4 p.m. count."

"Alright. I better get back to work before I have another bout with Spits. He's been watching me like a hawk since I resumed this morning."

He started picking up the crap on the floor and headed towards the kitchen.

Chapter 17

DANNY KNEW HE COULD COUNT ON ASHA FOR INFORMATION. He was not surprised that Asha was the head of the Nigerian community in Petersburg. He had been sentenced to forty years in 1981 on a drug charge. That was the same year Danny was in London on a family trip. He was eight. He remembered it vividly, because that was the same year Lady Diana Spencer married Prince Charles of Wales. London was in a celebration mode. Evelyn had booked their flight to return to Nigeria on the same day, but all flights were cancelled at Heathrow airport.

Asha was seventeen years into his sentence and had recently downgraded from the maximum prison to the medium prison for good behavior. Over the years, Asha had built a vast network of contacts. Information was key for anyone who wanted to survive in prison.

Danny walked into the gym and saw Asha bench pressing 110 pounds on the Barbell considering his small stature.

"Hey Danny. What's up? Do you bench press?"

"Not really." Danny couldn't remember doing any weight lifting. The only reason he went to the gym before he got arrested was to womanize.

"Why don't you try something small like ten pounds while we chat."

"Alright. Any word?"

"Yes. I've got good news and bad news. The story going around is that you snitched on the B-More Boys and their New York affiliates in exchange for your reduced sentence. They feel retribution is warranted in your case."

"This is funny."

"This is not a joke Danny. These guys are serious business. The last guy who crossed them was carried out in a body bag just last month, even though he was transferred to Petersburg from a prison in upstate New York for his protection."

"I don't mean funny literarily. First, I did not snitch on anybody, even though the AUSA tried to turn me into an informant, while promising the moon and the stars. I turned him down and took my chances. If it wasn't for God who gave me favor before the judge, I would be doing a stretch just like you."

Asha was taken aback by his careless slip.

"Sorry no offense," he added. "It seems I can't win with these guys."

"None taken. I'm impressed. I guess I'm not the only one sourcing for information around here, he said with a smile."

"So, what's the good news?" asked Danny.

"Well, the B-More Boys are a very disciplined and structured gang, which is rare. They don't usually act unless there is a unanimous consensus of the leaders in each hall, most especially their leader, Reginald Beufort III. A native of Louisiana, convicted on a drug charge for conspiracy to distribute which earned him life sentence. However, the appeals court commuted his sentence to 15 years due to a legal technicality. He graduated from Princeton with an MBA. He is from a respected family and claims he doesn't believe in violence, though he has been alleged to have given the order for the murder of at least five potential government witnesses willing to testify against him. One of the murders took place right in Lee Hall just last year."

"I thought you said you had good news."

"Don't you see? It means they are very thorough. Which means you can make your case face to face."

"I don't like the sound of it, but I don't think I have much of a choice either. I need to stay ahead of this. How do you propose we go about this?"

"We need to set-up a meet with Reginald. I know him cordially and out of respect, we stay out of each other's way. He is housed at Virginia Hall. We need to find someone very close to him and well respected, and I think I know who."

"Who?" asked Danny anxiously.

"Aren't you a member of the choir at the chapel?"

"Yeah, but I just joined the group."

"That's fine. One of the deacons is a guy called Hailey. Nice guy and a wonderful Christian brother. He's Jamaican and on a twenty-five-year stretch. He used to be a member and a leader of the B-More Boys until he gave his life to Christ. To be honest, I don't know how they let him live. Usually, the only way out of that gang is through a body bag. We can ask for his audience and see if he can broker the meeting."

"Thank you so much, Asha. I really appreciate everything you've done for me. Also, I would like to take this opportunity to thank you for the job in the kitchen."

"What are you talking about? I didn't have anything to do with that."

"Do you think ....? asked Danny with a puzzled look"

"If I'm thinking, what you are thinking, then we need to get you in front of Reggie ASAP."

IT HAD BEEN OVER TWO WEEKS SINCE ASHA MADE CONTACT WITH Hailey about arranging the meeting with Reggie. Though Danny had seen Reggie a few times at the recreational yard and the chow hall, he knew better than to approach him. Reggie moved around the prison with an entourage of at least six members. Danny had been constantly watching his back. He called Lynn every night to check-up on her and update her on his daily activities. So far, everything looked good. Fortunately, Pookie was also assigned to the morning shift in the kitchen, which meant Danny would not be going to work alone at dawn. The walk from Lee hall to the kitchen took about ten minutes and was along a dimly lit path. The perfect place to be ambushed with no witnesses. Danny had developed a habit of praying and reading his Bible every morning. He was surprised to find that a lot of characters in the Bible, had also gone through times of persecution and betrayal. Nevertheless, they never lost their faith and Danny wasn't about to lose his faith either. It had brought him purpose in life and a measure of peace beyond his comprehension.

When Danny and Pookie walked into the chow hall to report for duty, Spits motioned them over.

"Good morning Jimmy."

"I hope it's a good morning for you, boy. Someone wants to see you in my office."

"Who?" asked Danny timidly.

"You've got thirty minutes. Make it count."

Danny glanced over at Pookie.

"You want me to come with you? asked Pookie. I've got your back."

"Sure. I appreciate it."

Pookie had gotten wind of the contract through the grapevine last week and was furious with him for not letting him know what was going on, despite being cell mates. Danny felt bad and assured him it had nothing to do with trust. He had been overwhelmed with the situation from the start and had felt this was his problem to fix alone. Danny told him about the situation. Pookie insisted that it was not safe to walk around alone on the prison premises. Danny hadn't expected such a gesture from Pookie since he was on his way home and had just seven months left on his sentence. Most inmates try to stay out of trouble to avoid the risk of losing their "good time" as their release date gets closer. Danny tried to convince him otherwise, but his resolve remained.

As they walked towards Spits' office, Danny saw Reggie's

entourage outside the door. One of them motioned to him to lift his hands for a pat down. These were common in the prison, despite multiple unannounced shakedowns by the authorities. Weapons were easily replaceable. Inmates could make a shank out of anything. Danny had witnessed an inmate with a shank made from the blade of a shaving stick bought from the commissary, and another inmate, who quickly grabbed his toothbrush and grazed the handle on the concrete floor till the edge was sharp, pointed and ready for battle.

Danny never knew if Pookie was armed. He knew not to ask questions. After the inmate patted Danny down, he looked over his shoulder.

"Who's is with you?" he asked.

"A friend," Danny replied.

"I will have to pat him down also."

"Nobody is patting me down," said Pookie in a husky voice as he walked closer to the entourage.

Reggie opened the door.

"Are you Danny?"

"Yes, I am."

"Come in. Just you," he said as he motioned to Pookie to stop.

Danny walked into the office, his fingers trembling.

"I'm not going to hurt you. If I wanted you dead, we would not be having this conversation right now. I'm here as a courtesy to brother Hailey who vouched for you as an outstanding member of the church. I can't remember the last time he vouched for anyone. You must be special. Would you like some coffee?"

"I'm good," said Danny. He wondered at how Reggie drank with ease from the flask in the lunchbox of Spits as if they were colleagues or family friends. This should not be a surprise, thought Danny. According to Asha, most of the officers in Petersburg were on the payroll of the B-More Boys and it seemed Spits was not an exception. Reggie had a calm demeanor and was soft spoken as if he were in corporate boardroom for a meeting.

"Look man", said Danny abruptly. "I did not snitch on you guys. You can check my court transcripts at the courthouse. Someone is trying to frame me."

"Take it easy Danny. I believe you. I already saw your transcripts."

"You did?" said Danny.

"Sure. I'm very thorough and a proponent of due diligence before I make any decision. I had our lawyers check it out which is why it took this long for me to accept this meeting."

"If you knew I was innocent, you could just have disregarded my request or asked brother Hailey to convey your message."

Danny sat straight on the chair Spits had nick named "The Flush". The chair had earned its nick name as a passage to solitary, also known as, "the hole". Whenever Spits asked to see an inmate who'd disobeyed a direct order, he either gave you a warning or his fingers were already on the panic button for the goon squad in full battle gear to arrest you and send you to the hole. Danny had experienced this first hand. One day after his shift ended, Danny was looking forward to his favorite daytime soap *The Young & the Restless.* Spits said he was shorthanded and needed him to stay on for another two hours. Danny refused. Jimmy asked to see Danny in his office and asked Danny to sit in that chair. Five minutes later, the siren went off in the yard and all inmates were instructed to lay flat on the floor, facedown wherever they were. Danny was admitted into the hole and sentenced by the warden to two weeks and loss of visitation and phone privileges.

"I see," said Danny with a puzzled look. "You have the same nagging question that had been bothering me, and you were hoping I could provide the answer."

"I'm not sure what you mean."

"Sure, you do. I've been asking myself, why me? Why would anybody want to frame me? I've been asking the wrong question."

"And what is the right question?" asked Reggie.

"The question is, who has much to gain if I cooperate with the government to testify against you and the B-More Boys?"

"And?"

"Hold on a minute. I can't speak for your organization's activities. If we are both convicted already for unrelated crimes, then someone out there wants you to deliver on their expectation. They were not counting on your capacity to be shrewd, structured and thorough before taking action."

"I guess I should take that as a compliment. I'm not following you."

"Don't you understand? Someone out there wants to make a statement and it looks like we are pawns on a grand scale of a chess game."

"Any suggestions?"

"Not sure yet, but I think I have a plan to find out who is behind this."

Danny heard three knocks on the door. It was one of Reggie's boys. Time to wrap up.

"I have a feeling I'm going to like you Danny. You were not what I expected."

"I hope so. I will take that as a compliment." Danny replied. He didn't want to know what he'd expected.

"Alright, you can go. You know how to reach me."

Danny opened the door, walked towards Pookie and quickly disappeared into the kitchen.

Chapter 18

IT WAS ABOUT 7 P.M. WHEN JOHN ROSENBERG AND HIS WIFE SHERYLL pulled into the basement parking lot of the Hyatt Regency Hotel in Washington D.C. This was a fundraiser event sponsored by the Republican Party. John hated these kind of gatherings, where you are expected to shake hands with people you detested just to get what you wanted. A bunch of hypocrites, he thought. If only he could see through their souls, he would surely find a dagger somewhere in their hearts.

On the other hand, Sheryll had been looking forward to this event. She had at least two hundred business cards with her and planned to find new clients for her catering business. The party would be attended by the crème de la crème of the D.C. socialites and politicians. As much as he would have preferred staying home to watch the Redskins play the Dallas Cowboys, John could not deny his father's request. Senator Gregory Rosenberg was not a man you said no to. A former Marine, staunch conservative and a political wonk. He had been a United States Senator representing the State of Maryland for most of John's life.

They pulled up into a parking lot. John fidgeted with his bow tie, as Sheryll checked her make-up and glossed her lips one more time. John could feel his tongue strapped to the roof of his mouth. He was thirsty and needed a drink to calm his nerves.

"Let me help you with your tie," said Sheryll.

"I told him I don't want his help to go into politics, but he thinks I'm just having the jitters. Just because he loves being a politician, does not mean I have to follow in his footsteps".

"Look John! Your dad only wants what is best for you. Don't

blow it for everyone."

"Thanks for all the support."

"I'm just saying, it might not be as bad as you think. Let's just enjoy the night. Come on!"

When the French doors opened, John saw many familiar faces. He walked through the crowd shaking hands. He saw the senator at the end of the hall holding a glass of wine and chatting with a group of lobbyists. He hoped that was the first glass. His dad had developed a drinking problem over the past five years after his mum had passed away. They've had interventions and checked him into a rehab clinic, but he constantly relapsed. John partly blamed himself when his father started drinking, but everyone thought it was a temporary phase to deal with the pain of his wife's death. Mum had been his rock. The family had been surprised when he got re-elected despite the low poll numbers and his opponent assassinating his character daily regarding his alcohol abuse. Most people thought he was lucky, but John knew better. The senator was savvy and understood the public would sympathize with him as a widower as long as his opponent campaigned with negative ads. His opponent was young and inexperienced.

John approached the senator, interrupting his conversation with a hug.

"Hello dad."

"Hi kiddo. How are ya? Where is Sheryll?"

"I lost her in the crowd when we walked in," he said in a hush tone feeling embarrassed.

"At least, you can't deny the fact that she knows what she wants. Hey guys, you remember my son John? He is the U.S. Attorney for the U.S District Court, Greenbelt Division that I 've been talking to you about."

"Yes", said one of the senator's major donors. "Your dad has been telling us about your ambition to run in the Maryland gubernatorial election next year."

"Yeah. I'm still mulling over it."

"He's being modest. We need to talk," said the senator abruptly.

As John waved to the group, the senator grabbed his arm and walked him into an empty room, locking the door behind him.

"What are you doing? Why would you tell them you're still mulling over it? Do you know how much political capital I've spent convincing the party that you are the right candidate to be the next governor of Maryland?"

"I did not ask for any of this. This is your dream and not mine."

"Well, it's too late. Donations have already started streaming in by the major players and bailing out now will not look good for you. Your job is on the line."

"What? Are you kidding me? I love my job. Has it ever occurred to you maybe I'll even be more of an embarrassment running for an office I could care less about? This is more about your reputation, not mine."

"Look here boy! You might not agree with me on my approach in life, but take it from me, this is good for you. How many times have I heard you talk about how messed up the criminal justice system is and how gangs are just having their way with innocent victims? What better way to fix things by being a governor instead of crying about it. Now, man up and get to work."

John sat down overwhelmed. He ran his hands through his hair.

"Now what?" asked John.

"You need a breakthrough arrest and convictions that are worthy of the media's attention. The last time we spoke, I thought we agreed that cleaning up Maryland by arresting the B-More Boys was your ticket and your way out. Whatever happened to the potential witness you had in your custody who knows the inner workings of this gang?"

"His name is Danny Adeyinka. My office offered him time served and his deportation waived in conjunction with the USCIS., but he declined. That took us by surprise. It was a sweet deal. A get out of jail free card. We offered him another plea deal of three years, no strings attached, hoping Judge Machete would deny the deal as he has done plenty of times in the past. To our amazement, he went along with the deal and we had no grounds to object."

"We have to do something," said the senator. "This guy is perfect. A convicted undocumented immigrant living in the U.S for a decade and defrauding innocent victims. This is the narrative the party is counting on. I think it's time to tighten the screw on this guy."

"What are you suggesting?"

"I'm not suggesting anything. Let's say hypothetically, if the life of this inmate is threatened by the B-More Boys, would it be feasible to presume his cooperation with your office?"

"Not going to work. Let's just say a rumor was released last month into the prison population about the inmate snitching on the B-More Boys. Our expectation was that there could be a reprisal against the inmate, but so far everything has been silent".

"Well then, why don't you use your imagination. It's time to up the ante and tighten the screws. In my experience, that never fails. C'mon, everyone will be wondering where we are, and I need a drink."

They opened the door, and Sheryll waved John over. She needed him beside her as she made the rounds. John was always amazed how she worked the floor with grace and style in the world politics and hypocrisy he found himself.

JOHN ARRIVED AT THE COURTHOUSE BUILDING AT 6 A.M TO GET AN EARLY START. He'd been tired all weekend. The fundraiser had taken a toll on his body. He drank more than usual to numb himself, while Sheryll dragged him all over the place. He slept through the day on Sunday, though he had planned to work on some cases from home over the weekend. The conversation he had with the senator was on his mind. He had never been this frustrated over a case, especially one so significantly tied to his career.

John could not shake the feeling that the senator was right. This was the time to strike and run for governor. Democrats had held the position more times than their Republican counterparts. The party is backing him based on his last name and the current political climate. People were starting to feel uncomfortable with the number of immigrants pouring into their cities, the steady rise in crime and gang activities. The party felt there was no better candidate than the U.S. Attorney to make the case to the American people. It was time for the Republicans to take back control of the state, an opportunity that if missed, would not come around again for a while.

There was a knock on the door. Edward Reese popped his head in.

"Good morning boss. You wanted to see me?"

"Come in, Edward. How are you and the family?"

"We are great, sir."

"Good. Have a seat. Do you want some coffee?"

"Sure," he said with a curious look on his face.

John poured him a cup from a fresh batch he'd made. Usually Nikki, his secretary made the coffee, but she does not resume till eight o'clock.

"So, how is the case regarding the B-More Boys going? Are you making any headway?"

"The situation as at the last time we spoke remains at status quo, said Edward Reese looking puzzled." He had updated his boss last week on the case, explaining to him that the B-More Boys had not taken the bait concerning Danny Adeyinka. The impression he got at the end of that meeting from John was to put a halt on the investigation until there was another opportunity to re-open the case against the gang. He wasn't sure what to make of the questions this morning, unless his boss knew something he didn't.

"Are you telling me there is no other way to make this work? asked John."

"No sir. At least, for now."

"How long have you worked for me Edward? He relaxed on the new office chair Nikki had ordered for him last week.

"Five years sir."

"Off the record. Let me clear things up and paint a bigger picture for you. Though I've not announced my intentions to run for governor, the party has given me the green light to be their nominee for the coming elections."

"That's great boss. Congratulations!"

"Thanks, but that was the good news. Here is the bad news. My chances of winning are slim to none if I can't clean up the crime ridden streets of Baltimore and its surrounding suburbs. How do I convince the people of the great state of Maryland that I am up to the challenge of managing the state when I can't even get rid of the B-More Boys and reduce the crime rate? The party's position this election cycle is to be tough on crime and illegal immigration. They are counting on me."

John paused for a minute, and then continued.

"Do you have any ambition outside of this office, Edward?"

"Yes, I do. Hopefully in the private sector if the opportunity presents itself."

"Let me remind you, just in case you forgot. Upon my formal announcement, the U.S. Attorney General will need to send my replacement, who might not take kindly to you since he doesn't know who you are and does not have your trust. Hence, this office will experience a serious shuffle of staff. I can't promise you that you will not be a casualty, but I can take you along with me. How about the Chief of Staff to the Governor of Maryland?"

"Sounds great sir. Has a good ring to it."

"In that case, why don't you see to it to convince Mr. Adeyinka to become a confidential informant for this office."

"In exchange for what? said Edward. We don't have any more leverage to bargain with him and he has made it clear that he is not going to sell anybody out. He just wants to accept responsibility for the crimes he committed and do his time."

John got up from his chair and walked towards his window overlooking the park. He could see people walking their dogs and little kids on the swings.

"You will be amazed how people can change their minds when their lives are in danger."

"Not sure I follow sir," said Edward.

"Don't we have an informant from the El-Rino gang also locked up at the prison in Petersburg?"

"Not sure sir. I'll look into it."

"I hear there is a vicious rivalry between those groups for dominance within those walls. It would be a pity if Mr. Adeyinka is caught in the middle. Don't you think, Edward?"

"Yes sir. It would be a shame."

"Well then, I expect to hear some good news very soon. You have a good day Edward."

"Good day sir."

Edward Reese walked out of the office just as Nikki opened the door with the daily newspapers in hand. She was ready to make the coffee for the U.S Attorney just as she had done every day for the past five years.

Chapter 19

IT HAD BEEN TWO WEEKS SINCE DANNY'S MEETING
with Reginald Beufort in Spits' office. He had been praying
fervently for an answer to the nagging question they'd con-
cluded with the meeting. Certainly, he was appreciative for
being alive everyday. Life had been normal so far in the prison
yard, especially now that Reggie knew he was the ultimate target
and he was the prospective bait. At least it was comforting to
know that the gang was very disciplined, as Asha had predicted.

Nevertheless, Danny watched his back. Pookie had been a
huge source of support, walking with him to work just to lessen
the chances of anyone getting funny ideas. As much as Danny
appreciated the gesture, he thought it would be a shame if anything happened to Pookie when he had two weeks left before
going home. Not on my watch, Danny thought. After one of
many workouts and updates of the on-going situation with Reggie and the B-More Boys at the recreation center, Danny asked
Asha for a work transfer. He wanted to work as a cleaner in Lee
Hall where he resides. He figured it was safer for him and
Pookie. The job entailed cleaning the hallways when the inmates
had gone to their jobs in the yard. Pookie would not be obligated
to escort him to work. He expected to finish all his chores
quickly, with enough time left over to read his Bible and watch
The Young & the Restless.

After his soap opera, the news came on, showing John Rosenberg, the U.S. Attorney for the United States District Court,
Southern District, Greenbelt Division at a news conference. Behind him were couple of his assistants and some detectives. He

discussed whether there would be charges brought against a former FBI agent, who shot an innocent by-stander during a shootout with the B-More Boys gang on a routine raid on an alleged compound believed to be the one of the drug houses used by the gang to transact drug deals. Danny walked a little closer to the TV screen and recognized Edward Reese and agent Ramirez. Suddenly it dawned on him.

This is why they've been coming at me all this while, he muttered under his breath. I'm the golden goose for the U.S Attorney. Danny remembered agent Ramirez's comments to his colleague in the cruiser after his arrest. Ramirez had told his colleague not to worry, that "the U.S Marshals will wait for this one. They have their instructions. They have no choice." After that, Edward Reese and Ramirez tried to railroad him with subtle threats at the Charles County Detention Center to convince him to be an informant and testify against the B-More Boys. "It didn't make sense at the time, but now it's all clear to me," said Danny to himself. All roads led to the governor's mansion in Annapolis. Danny grabbed his glasses and made haste to his cell. He had to speak to Reggie.

The chow hall was full today, thought Danny. Fried rice and a quarter chicken were on the menu. Either Spits was in a good mood or the warden had decided to patronize the inmates to reduce tension and hostility in the yard. Amazingly, this technique was very effective, especially after a radical unscheduled shakedown of the halls by the warden had resulted in a huge loss of contraband costing the inmates thousands of dollars. Also, the bus had arrived with about two hundred inmates from various county jails and detention centers to start their sentences. Eating rice and baked chicken allowed the inmates to reminisce like they were back home.

Danny looked for Reggie as the queue moved at a slow pace. He had sent an urgent message to Reggie asking for an immediate audience. So far, Reggie had been careful not to be seen with Danny in public. He still had a reputation to uphold and the rumor going around still posed a threat to his credibility as the leader of the B-More Boys. Suddenly, Spits appeared from the kitchen, just as it was Danny's turn to get his chicken.

"Hey Jimmy, what's up? Can a brother get a double portion today?"

"You don't work for me anymore. Remember, you resigned couple of months ago to be a cleaner in Lee Hall. How's that working out for you?"

"You wouldn't understand Jimmy. You've always treated me nice and I appreciate it, but being alive takes precedent over the benefits of the working in the kitchen."

"No worries Danny! I've sorted you out already. It's in my office. Why don't you go and get it?" he said with a smirk.

"Sure", said Danny hesitantly. He could read between the lines. Either Reggie was waiting for him, or this might be the end of his life. Danny had to trust his instincts. He had asked for this meeting and there was no going back. He sighed with relief when he saw Reggie having his meal in Spits office without his bodyguards. Either the chicken must be great, or Reggie had gained Danny's trust after all.

"Have a seat," Reggie said as he wiped his mouth with a cloth napkin. He used cutlery with the initials R.B on the handle. Danny sat comfortably on "The Flush" without a second thought. This is déjà vu, he thought.

"So, I trust you have an update. You have my attention."

"I figured it out and I need your help."

"Figured what out?"

"I'm the golden goose Reggie. This is not just about reigning in your gang because of its nefarious activities on the streets. Sorry, no offense!"

"None taken. Please continue."

"This is about the road leading to the governor's mansion in Annapolis."

"I'm not following."

"The U.S Attorney has waged a war with the B-More Boys for political credibility. Just found out that John Rosenberg is running for governor on the Republican ticket. The party's focus this year is crime reduction and illegal immigration"

"This is nothing new Danny. The Republicans have been pushing the same agenda for years."

"Don't you get it? He needs a conviction that will generate enough media attention for his campaign. Though you are here for a fifteen-year sentence with just three years to go, he needs me to bring a bigger charge against you that carries a life sentence to seal your fate. A life sentence that will leave you vulnerable and create mutiny within your ranks."

"You are not helping yourself here Danny. You are backing up the opinion of some of my boys to take you out and neutralize the threat. They might just have a point from what you just told me."

"I see you don't get it. Either dead or alive, I will be the reason for your great downfall. I'm sure the good U.S Attorney has redundancy plans in place, watching your every move within these walls. What do you think will happen to you when they find out about the secret meetings you've had with me? If anything happens to me, you are toast. On the other hand, I'm sure the office of the U.S Attorney will use any means necessary to make sure my life is under threat whether by you or a rival gang and hope I will be forthcoming to make a deal to give you up when that happens. I can assure you, I'm not that stupid. That's a promise you can count on. I've demonstrated that in the past."

Reggie sighed.

"What do you suggest?"

"I think it is better for both of us if our common threat is eliminated."

"How?" Reggie asked leaning forward, like a student ready to learn.

"First, by closing all roads to Annapolis. I presume you have connections with the officers at reception, right?"

"Yeah! Tell them to lookout for a visit from Agent Ramirez. We need to find out who they are talking to. It's time to stop playing defense. Wait for further instructions. I've got to go. I'm famished. There is a double portion of rice and chicken with my name on it waiting for me."

Danny walked out of Spits' office emboldened. He strutted back to the chow hall with his cutlery in hand to do battle with the chicken.

AFTER THE TWELVE O'CLOCK COUNT, Danny was getting ready to watch his favorite daytime soap opera when he heard officer Matthew's voice from the intercom.

Danny Adeyinka, you have a visitor.

Danny had been waiting for this call for the past two weeks. It had to be his lawyer. Just after his daily morning prayers and devotion, he got the idea to get in touch with Susan Macarthy, his court appointed lawyer. Though his case was over, he was not sure if she would be willing to represent him again. At this point, she was the only one he could trust to give him advice.

Every weekend, Lynn had been to the prison to visit him. Danny counted himself blessed to have her in his life again. Once he was reading his Bible and he stumbled on the scripture in the book of Proverbs, chapter eighteen and verse twenty-two, which describes how a person who finds a good wife finds a good thing and obtains favor from the Lord. It makes a lot of sense, he thought, because he didn't deserve her. Danny made the effort to keep her apprised of the situation in the prison while trying his best not to get her worried. During the visit two weeks ago, he'd had to open up to her about the threats over his life and the plan of the U.S Attorney. For a while, she sobbed, but Danny calmed her down.

"What do we do now?" she asked wiping tears from her eyes.

"I have a plan, but I need you to stay focused replied Danny. I need you to reach out to my lawyer. Her name is Susan Macarthy. Here is her business card. Preferably, call her mobile."

"Would it not be better if you called her directly? She doesn't know who I am."

"Absolutely not, Danny replied. First, you know all our calls are monitored. Second, not sure she would like to accept my call. Third, this is something I need to discuss with her in person. I have a plan to derail the political agenda of a United States Attorney. This is serious business."

"What exactly do you want me to tell her?"

"Tell her, I need to talk to her in-person, it is matter of life and death and it is related to my case."

"Would they allow her to see you?"

"Sure. She is still my lawyer as long as the matter at hand is related to my case."

"Okay. I'll call her on Monday."

"One more thing," said Danny. If she agrees to see me, just say the word "green" and if not, just say "red".

"Okay. How about you spend some quality time with me. Visit will be over in the next two hours."

"Yes ma'am," he replied.

She smiled.

OFFICER MATTHEW USHERED Danny into the interview room next to prison reception. Susan sat with her back to the door. He could recognize her scruffy blonde hair. She still looked the same, except for the worried look on her face. Danny was sure, she'd been shocked when Lynn approached her on his behalf.

"Hello Danny. How are you?"

"Hi Susan. I'm fine. Thanks for asking. You look great."

"Thanks. I'm curious though. Why am I here? A lady named Lynn called me and told me I had to come see you. That it was a matter of life and death. I thought she was exaggerating, but she convinced me.

"Are you still my lawyer? I need to know if everything we discuss is still protected by the privilege?"

"I'm still your lawyer if you want me to be, especially when it relates to your case. Which means everything we discuss is privileged."

"Good. I need your help Susan. The ink is already dry on the contract placed on my head by the U.S Attorney to achieve his political ambition at any cost. As far these guys are all concerned, I'm just collateral damage."

"These guys?" Susan asked in a hush tone.

"Yes. The office of the U.S. Attorney is compromised and being used as a tool to threaten the lives of inmates and drive the agenda of the Republican party."

"This is crazy Danny. Do you hear yourself? Do you have any proof?"

"No," said Danny as he leaned back in his chair, frustrated. Tears rolled down his cheeks.

"I'm sorry Danny. I didn't mean to upset you, but if what you are saying is correct I don't see how I can help you. If you are going to accuse the U.S. Attorney, we have to have compelling evidence or else we would be the laughing stock of the entire legal community. Let's not even talk about me losing my job at the firm, knowing some of the senior partners are friends with John Rosenberg and his father."

For a few minutes, there was silence between them. Though Susan empathized with Danny, seeing how scared and nervous he was, she couldn't seem to think of any way to help him. Suddenly, Danny raised his head from the table.

"Do you have any contacts at the U.S. District Court, Northern District in Baltimore?"

"Yes! I have a friend who is an assistant U.S. attorney over there."

"Do you trust him?" asked Danny.

"Yes. I've known him for over five years. He was my former boyfriend."

"Was the break-up mutual or hostile?"

"That's none of your business."

"No offense here. Just need to know if he has your back. No one can see us coming if this is to work. Some of his colleagues probably worked in the southern district office. So, you can see my concern."

"If what is to work?" she said.

Danny leaned forward. Though their conversation was privileged, he might still get killed in here for what he says.

"We have been informed that agent Ramirez has visited this prison to see an inmate, a guy from the El-Rino gang."

"First, what do you mean "we"? Secondly, how did you get that information?"

"I'm getting some help from an inmate. His name is Reginald Beaufort."

"What? Isn't he the notorious gang leader of the B-More Boys who you claim the U.S attorney initially wanted you to inform on? You guys are friends now?"

"Yes. That's a long story and the answer to your second question."

Susan raised her hands and said, "I don't want to know".

"Anyways, said Danny. You can verify the information from the visitor's log on your way out."

"Let's just say hypothetically that your information is correct. Ramirez has a right to come here to see any inmate he wants at any time. There is nothing suspicious about that."

"True. However, we have first hand information that the inmate's wife was arrested last year, and she is looking at fifteen years for a drug offense attached to a deportation order to Mexico. Furthermore, we know Ramirez was not the arresting officer of the wife's case. So why has he been here to visit this inmate four times this month? I'm telling you Susan, this is the guy they are employing to engage the B-More Boys and at the same time set me up to roll the dice on the gang. Which means my life is over either way and it's a win-win for the U.S attorney or the future governor of Maryland."

"So, what do you want me to do?" she asked.

"Ask your friend at the northern district, to check the file on an inmate named Carlito Morales, a Mexican national on a thirty-year sentence, convicted seven years ago."

"Okay. I've got to get back to the office. I'll get back to you immediately if I find something. Please stay safe."

"Don't worry, God is on my side and He will see me through."

"I'm glad you are still holding to your faith. I've been going to church more often too, since the day you got convicted. I rededicated my life to Christ."

"That's nice Susan. Really happy for you."

"Okay. Talk to you later."

"Sure. Please watch your back."

"Will do", she said as she knocked on the door. It was opened by officer Matthew who was finishing a sandwich. Susan walked towards the reception and disappeared from Danny's view.

Chapter 20

IT HAD BEEN RAINING ALL NIGHT as forecasted. Susan woke up feeling tired. She applied her eyeliner and wondered why she had butterflies in her stomach at the thought of seeing Jonas Malone for lunch at Café Catfish in downtown Baltimore. She'd last seen him there over two years ago. Instead of proposing marriage, as she'd expected, he told her he'd been offered a position at the U.S. Attorney's office at the Northern District of Texas in Dallas. He wanted her opinion. She hurried out of the café crying and never looked back. Jonas had made several attempts to reach her, but she avoided him at every opportunity. She heard later through the grapevine that he turned down the offer in Dallas. Looking back, she felt petty and stupid about losing the only man she had ever loved over her selfish desire and pride. He was probably married now, living in one of the fancy houses in Baltimore.

Suddenly, her intercom came alive. Her taxi was ready downstairs. She grabbed her umbrella, keys and briefcase and dashed out the door.

At the café. Jonas was seated close to the window overlooking the harbor. A couple of fishing boats went in and out of the harbor, a little bit unusual for this time of the year, but Jonas could care less. All his attention was on Susan as she stepped out of the taxi. Her smile hadn't changed.

"How are you Susan?" He stood up to greet her.

"I'm fine Jonas. You look great," she said staring at his left hand to confirm what she had dreaded all along.

"Same to you, Susan."

Silence fell.

"I have a client who is in trouble and I need your help," she said after downing the tonic water Jonas had ordered for her. It was her favorite.

"You don't waste any time, do you?"

"Sorry, I was parched". She signaled the waiter and ordered another glass.

"How can I help you?" Jonas said. He was disappointed. He'd hoped she'd wanted to see him for personal reasons, not professional ones.

"Do you know Edward Reese?"

"Sure. We've worked together on couple of cases. What about him?"

"Can you find out if he ever prosecuted a case involving an inmate called Carlito Morales or any of his family members? He is currently housed at F.C.I. Petersburg. He is a Mexican national on a thirty-year sentence, convicted seven years ago for murder and aggravated assault. If not, can you find out who the arresting agent was for the case?"

"What is this about?" he asked.

"I think for now, it's better you don't know. This is as a result of a privileged information from my client".

"What have you gotten yourself into? Do you know what you're asking me to do? Snooping around on colleagues like this can be seen as a real betrayal, which could destroy trust and opportunities for future cooperation, including my career."

"Fine. Forget I asked. This was a mistake," she said attempting to get up.

Jonas took her hand. "I never said I won't help. I should have what you need in a few days. I still have about thirty minutes left on my lunch break. Why don't we catch up?"

Susan placed her briefcase back on the floor next to her and asked him what he wanted to know. Suddenly, those butterflies in her stomach started rattling again.

"Are you married or in a relationship?" Jonas asked nervously.

"No. I've been busy at work and hadn't had the time to date since I became a junior partner at the firm.

"Congratulations. I'm happy for you. You deserved it. That's all you've talked about since we met in college."

"Thanks. What about you?"

"I'm not married. I've had trouble trusting any woman since you walked out of my life. I couldn't understand what happened to us. I thought we were in a good place to take our relationship to the next level, which was why I wanted your opinion when I was offered the job in Texas. I wanted us to make that decision together if we were going to get married."

"Married? She asked as tears rolled down her cheeks."

"Oh, have I upset you? I don't want to lose you again."

"No. I'm the one who should apologize Jonas. I'm sorry."

Jonas got up from his seat to console her. He hugged her and wiped her tears with his hankie.

I have an idea. How about we start all over? asked Jonas.

"I would love that," she said as she leaned forward and kissed him.

DANNY HAD BEEN MOPPING THE SAME SPOT for several minutes, wondering what had happened to Susan. He had tried to call her couple of times, but it always went to voice mail. It'd been over a week since they'd hatched a plot to go on the offensive. He would not be able to live with himself if anything happened to her. The idea of asking Lynn to contact her again was appealing, but Danny resolved not to involve her any more than he had to, just in case things went south. It was hard enough worrying about Susan. He felt a tap on his shoulder. He jolted and nearly lost his footing on the wet floor. It was Officer Matthew.

"Are you okay, Danny?"

"Yes. You surprised me, that's all."

"Sorry about that. You have a visitor. I believe your lawyer is here to see you."

Danny was relieved. She had probably avoided his calls in case anyone was listening, he thought. The fact that she is here meant she must have stumbled on something significant.

"Hello, Danny."

"Hi Susan. I trust all is well with you?" Susan looking over her shoulder as Officer Matthew closed the door. Her behavior confirmed Danny's suspicion that this was bigger than they might have anticipated." When she was sure the door was secured, she spoke.

"Sorry, I missed your calls, but I've been edgy since I started fishing into the case of Carlito Morales and boy, did we hit the motherload. Lately, I think someone has been following me."

"What? What did they look like?"

"I haven't seen anyone yet. It was a black, tinted Crown Victoria with government tags. However, I'm not sure. Maybe I'm just paranoid because of this case. Sometimes, I've wondered why I ended up with this case of all the cases the courthouse could have assigned. To make matters worse, I'm doing it pro-bono. My firm has started wondering why my billing hours have taken a nose dive. Danny Adeyinka! You owe me big time."

"There is no dispute in that regard. I really appreciate all your effort and diligence you've exacted on my behalf. God bless you. One day, I will repay you."

"Okay, okay!" she said blushing. "Let's get down to the issue at hand. Remember my friend at the Northern District U.S. attorney's office? "

"You mean your boyfriend?"

"Yes! No!" she said."

"Whatever you say." Danny grinned.

"He was able to find out who prosecuted Carlito and it definitely was not Edward Reese. Not only that, he was prosecuted in the Northern District."

"So, there is no connection? he said in disappointment."

"Not really."

"Sorry, what do you mean?"

"Just hear me out. I felt just the same way you are feeling right now when I got the news. However, I asked my friend to find out who the arresting agent was, and it was a DEA agent named Rodriguez Ramirez."

"Did you say Ramirez?" asked Danny.

"Your record didn't show you crossing paths with the DEA. Could there be another agent named Rodriguez Ramirez?"

"I didn't, but I believe we are both thinking of the same person. You never had the opportunity to meet him because I took a plea deal and never went to trial. Nevertheless, you should have recognized that name on my file and court records. He has to be the same agent who arrested me on these charges."

"I'm confused. Your file stated that Ramirez was a Secret Service Agent."

"Check the file. What year was Carlito arrested?"

Susan breezed through couple of documents in the file, "July 1987. Ten years ago. He must have transferred to the secret service not long after that. Now, this is making some sense. We know he is using Carlito's wife as leverage, but I don't see how he can make a deal when he has no jurisdiction. Her case is being prosecuted by the Northern District and it was a DEA bust."

"It could be a façade," Danny said as he paced the room. I'm sure they intend to string him on and pull the rug right from under him after he has done their bidding. They know he can't do anything. He is already serving a thirty-year sentence. Agent Ramirez and everyone involved all the way to John Rosenberg will deny any accusation unequivocally. I mean…. What is the word of a convicted criminal against a U.S Attorney? Nobody will believe him." Is there anything else? He put his hands on his head and squatted with his back against the wall."

"I think we have something here," said Susan as she turned over a piece of paper. "It looks like there have been couple of complaints and allegations against agent Ramirez for the past ten years. According to the Public Integrity Special Investigation Unit of the U.S Attorney's office, charges of corruption, murder-for-hire and witness tampering were dropped because witnesses, mostly inmates, either recanted or were found dead. So far, all the evidence they had has been circumstantial."

"What if I can get the U.S. Attorney's Office the evidence they need? Do you think they will take my case seriously? Especially, if it goes all the way to the top and one of their own."

"I don't see why not? I've met Martha Jenkins once or twice and have heard a lot about her. Before she became the U.S Attorney for the northern district, she was Assistant District Attorney for the southern district of New York. She is a stickler for rules and has zero tolerance for corrupt public and government officials. She did not hesitate to bust a ring of corrupt federal agents on the payroll of the Mafia bosses in New York, even though it was a public relations nightmare. In fact, this was the reason she was brought to Baltimore to clean house."

"Great," said Danny as he sat back down on his chair, excited.

"So, do you want me to make a formal complaint with the U.S Attorney's office at the northern district? If so, how do you propose we proceed? You know there is no going back. Don't forget, these are powerful people and this could go all the way to the Senate. This is a risky approach."

"Don't worry about me. Actually, I'm very concerned about your safety. Also, this could have adverse effect on you, your firm and your career. It leaves you vulnerable. However, I know it is risky and a long shot, but we have no choice. It's my only way out of this mess. I either wait for what is coming, which is a death warrant either way you look at it, or I take them on the offense. Can you get a meeting with Ms. Jenkins to make the formal complaint?

"Sure. Can I ask how you intend on getting the evidence?"

"I can't tell you just yet. Everything will depend on the co-operation of the U.S. Attorney's office. If they take the bait, I can assure you I will do whatever it takes to get what is needed for a successful prosecution and the derailment of the Rosenberg's political ambition and the Republican Party. I refuse to become anyone guinea pig."

"Oh! Look at the time. I've got to go. I'm late for a meeting with another client."

Danny leaned forward and held her hand. "It is well. Everything will be okay. Can I suggest you get the tag number of the car you think is following you? We can't afford to be careless and overlook anything at this point. Again, thanks for everything."

Susan got up quickly and tapped on the door. She walked quickly towards the reception and in a minute, she was out of sight.

Chapter 21

FROM THE WINDOW IN HIS CELL, Danny could barely make out the cars passing by the highway that ran near to the prison. He took solace watching people go about their daily activities after his morning devotion of prayer and Bible study. It was a reminder to stay focused and to keep trusting God. He would come out of this mess alive.

Life had not been the same since Pookie got released. He had been a great support and Danny could use his help right about now. Especially during the meeting sometime today with the leader of the El-Rino gang, which was brokered by Reginald Beaufort on behalf of the B-More Boys. When Danny first arrived at Petersburg, Asha had explained in great detail the unseen territorial lines dividing the prison into boroughs and the bureaucracy involved in crossing those lines without leaving the prison in a body bag. Danny was glad he'd paid attention. The prison siren went off indicating the end of count time and a call for chow time.

At first, Reggie would not agree to broker the meeting because he taught it was suicidal and highly unusual. He was worried what his boys would think of him in such a compromising position. But, Danny made the case that this meeting was absolutely necessary and of great benefit to all parties involved. If the U.S. Attorney was going to take the bait, Carlito Morales must turn against the same person promising freedom for his wife and family. Reggie knew better there was no way they could approach Carlito without getting the El-Rino leadership involved. Any course of action contrary to that would lead to an all-out war between the gangs. The last time both gangs were at odds, a couple of inmates lost their lives and it took the government two days to quell the riot.

Coincidentally, Lee hall, North Carolina and Virginia hall were released first for chow time. The smell of fried chicken, mashed potatoes and delicious vegetables wafted from the kitchen. Danny knew that everything had been carefully staged to distract the inmates in order to keep the recreational building empty. This has to be Spits' handiwork. Both gangs had chosen ten of their leaders to attend the meeting which included Danny, Carlito Morales, Reggie and Francisco Jose Miguel, the leader of the El-Rino gang. Everyone was patted down for weapons by the opposing gang members to guarantee the security and success of the meeting.

Francisco got up, raised his right hand and the room went silent. Turning to Reggie, he said "Okay. You called for this meeting esé. To be honest, we thought it was a ruse and probably you and your boys were up to no good. However, when you mentioned Carlito and the visits from agent Ramirez, we had to take your invitation serious because the specifics of the meetings were not known to anyone outside of this circle. The issue concerning Carlito, who is also my nephew, is of great concern to the gang and our families outside these walls. So, without any delay, what are you offering?"

"I will let Danny have the floor. He is the reason we are all here," said Reggie. He sat cross-legged, looking relaxed.

Danny felt his knees buckle. He was nervous and parched. However, he knew this was not the time to fumble. He cleared his throat.

"My name is Danny Adeyinka. I would just like to make a disclaimer. I'm not a member of the B-More Boys."

"We know who you are. Get to the point," said Francisco.

"It's come to our attention that agent Ramirez approached Carlito Morales in the past weeks to offer a service of either causing harm to me or getting rid of me and making sure the B-More Boys are framed for it, Reggie in particular. Also, we know that agent Ramirez has promised to drop the case against Carlito's wife in addition to putting a stop to her deportation back to Mexico. However, what you don't know is why he contracted you and I can assure you he has no intention of coming through on the deal."

"We don't need to know why," Francisco interrupted. El-Rino does not ask questions as long as El-Rino gets what it wants. Furthermore, why shouldn't we trust him? He has delivered in the past."

"That was when he was just a DEA agent," said Reggie. He could afford to look the other way for your drugs to flow into the country without inspections. Things have changed now, and he is hoping to pull this off on his past credit with the gang. Agent Ramirez is in the big leagues now and working for people who will not allow even the mention of your names to be associated with them. Don't you see? This is his retirement package and he is using you jokers to cash in his chips."

Danny stepped in to maximize the opening Reggie had created. "The only way agent Ramirez can guarantee that your wife will not be prosecuted and deported is through the office of the U.S. Attorney of the northern district in Baltimore which has the jurisdiction over her case. Do you have a written and signed agreement regarding this preposterous deal from the U.S. attorney's office? If you think I'm lying, why don't you ask agent Ramirez to provide you an agreement with the U.S. Attorney, and see if he comes through with it? I don't think he will" Danny replied.

Carlito went pale. He looked at Francisco. The gang leaders huddled together at the corner of the room and all Danny could hear was mutterings in Spanish and a lot of "Sí ese".

Reggie walked up behind him and whispered, "You've got them." Just then, they walked back towards Danny and

Francisco said, "Please tell me you didn't just come here to discourage us to forget about the whole thing, but you have something worthy to counter the agent's offer."

"Actually, I do," Danny said confidently. Looking straight at Carlito, he said, "What if I can get the case against your wife and her deportation dropped, guaranteed by a signed agreement with the U.S. Attorney's Office?"

"What do we have to do in exchange?" said Carlito.

"All you have to do is wear a wire the next time you speak to agent Ramirez and get him to incriminate himself by making him repeat what he has asked you to do."

"Wait a minute. Are you asking him to snitch on a federal agent?"

"Hey Papi, I don't think anyone in the gang or prison will be offended if I testify to bring down a corrupt agent, said Carlito abruptly. At least, we will be testifying against law enforcement for once. The gang and the inmates will celebrate us and give us an award if they can."

"Okay," said Francisco. "This is still my nephew we are talking about. I'm concerned for his wife's safety. What if agent Ramirez knows he is wearing a wire?"

"We are in prison Francisco," said Danny smiling. He was relaxed now. "Agent Ramirez will not see it coming, not even ten yards away. Here is what you do Carlito. When I give you the go ahead, call agent Ramirez and tell him you are not convinced on the deal and you need assurances. I'm optimistic, he'll return with a man named Edward Reese for support and that is when you will be wearing the wire."

The door to the recreation center flung open with both members of each gang assigned to be on the lookout outside the entrance gave the heads-up that inmates were approaching, and chow time was over.

Francisco approached Danny. "Okay esé, we have a deal. This better work or else I will personally castrate you."

"It's going to work. It's a win-win for everybody. Just to let you know, Jesus loves you and I love you too."

"You talk funny esé. You should consider being a comedian."

Everyone dispersed, and both gangs walked in opposite directions of the prison yard. Danny got back to his cell and got on his knees to thank God for the success of the meeting. He looked at his watch and rushed out to the phonebooth to call Lynn. They had an appointment for six o'clock and he was late.

SUSAN SAT IN THE WAITING ROOM NEXT TO MARTHA JENKINS OFFICE, drinking a cup of coffee and reading through the documents in her file. She had been there for the past hour with Jonas Malone waiting to see the U.S Attorney, who was in an ad-hoc meeting with the U.S. Attorney-General and could not be disturbed under any circumstances.

Susan and Jonas guessed the meeting was taking place because of the complaint she had filed with the Public Integrity Special Investigation Unit – the reason they were there that morning. Jonas had been instrumental in getting her the meeting on short notice. Susan was confident about the case. Lynn had contacted her over the weekend and let her know that Danny had secured the trust of Carlito Morales and the El-Rino gang. Carlito had decided to testify against agent Ramirez and become a witness for the federal government.

Susan had returned to Petersburg to get a written statement and permission to depose him with a video recorder in addition to his statement. Carlito Morales stated how agent Ramirez had asked him to murder a member of the B-More Boys and frame Danny Adeyinka for the crime. This would force Danny to testify against the B-More Boys. For this, Carlito's wife would be released, among future guarantees and protection for the gang's drug trade. Susan was very impressed with Danny. She wondered how he'd earned the trust of the El-Rino gang, but she knew better not to ask questions.

Just then, the Attorney-General walked out of Martha's office in a hurry with two other men in black suits. "Ms. Jenkins will see you now," said the secretary.

The office was spacious and bright with a lot of windows overlooking the harbor. The décor was simple. Martha stood elegantly by her desk and graciously offered each a soft handshake and gestured them to take a seat.

"Good morning" said Martha. "I'm so sorry about the delay."

"It's okay. We totally understand" said Susan.

"It was an unannounced visit by the Attorney-General regarding the complaint you filed and the allegations against agent Ramirez and my colleague in the southern district. I have been well briefed by Jonas and the director of the Public Integrity Special Investigation Unit. However, I don't have to tell you that these are serious allegations of corruption and abuse of power against the higher echelon of our Justice department, which is why it got the full attention of the Attorney-General. This is the first time my boss will come down to my office since I took over the northern district. Which means, we must tread carefully. Jonas informed me that you were able to depose the individual contracted to carryout the alleged atrocities mentioned in your complaint."

"Yes." Here are copies for your records."

"We need more evidence to corroborate the statements of Mr. Adeyinka and Mr. Morales before we can prosecute this case. The evidence must be convincing and irrefutable, considering your client and the informant are convicted criminals. There is no jury in the world that will take their words over a distinguished U.S. Attorney with an impeccable record. However, I have been authorized by my boss to create a unit to investigate the allegations. The unit will be comprised of individuals handpicked by me. These men and women have worked with me in the past with the utmost discretion, confidentiality and their records speak for themselves. I'm taking every effort to hedge this operation for the sake of justice and fairness. I don't want people's names to be tarnished if there is nothing here to pursue. Are you with me so far Ms. Macarthy?"

"Yes."

"My office will align itself with the plan you have embarked on for Mr. Morales to bait agent Ramirez for more assurances. We will take if from here. If we need anything else, Jonas will contact you. Thanks for coming."

"Thanks for accommodating me," said Susan.

"We are just doing our job. Jonas, can you stay behind?"

"Yes boss", said Jonas curiously.

Susan left, relieved. Things were progressing smoothly. She had planned on having to argue her case, but hadn't needed to. Danny's plan was working after all, she thought. As she waited for the elevator, Susan wondered why Martha asked Jonas to stay behind. She would ask him when he comes over for dinner later in the day.

Chapter 22

IT'S BEEN A BUSY WEEK FOR EDWARD REESE. He was on his way to see agent Ramirez. He walked to the café across the street from the United States Secret Service office. He hated going downtown during the rush hour, but Ramirez had insisted they meet in person because of some new development. Edward had been irritated by his phone call. What was so important that he could not handle it on his own? Ramirez had assured him that the El-Rino gang had always come through for him and they would owe him for guaranteed safe passage of all their drug trade throughout the state.

The city of Baltimore was highly coveted by gangs for the lucrative drug trade and high demand for narcotics. Currently the B-More Boys controlled the major market share. It should be an easy sell for the El-Rino gang to take advantage of the opportunity. The more Edward thought about it, the angrier he got. He had not had a good night's sleep for days. His in-laws were in town and he had a serious backlog of cases waiting for him at the office. He had never really liked Ramirez, but John had insisted on using him.

Edward entered the café and, saw Ramirez in the far corner waving him over.

"Have a seat," said Ramirez.

Edward hesitated, then sat down. A waitress came over to replace the sugar shaker on the table with a full jar and take his order.

"I'll have whatever he's having," said Edward.

"Why am I here Ramirez? We agreed not to be meeting like

this. What is it that you can't tell me over the phone? You had a little assignment to get your boys to do what we asked, in exchange for future guarantees. By now, my boss and I had thought we should be getting a phone call from Danny Adeyinka asking for protection or at least a murder file on my desk to prosecute Reginal Beaufort. You've delivered neither and you have the nerve to call me out of the office to have coffee and waste my time."

"Are you done?" asked Ramirez. "You think this easy. I didn't see this coming either. Like I told you, I've never had an issue with these guys. Look, I got a call from Carlito and went to see him at Petersburg. He is asking for assurances on paper that his wife's case will be dropped and she will not be deported. I tried to reason with him by asking him to check my record with gang. I told him I have always delivered and will do the same now. He still insisted he and the rest of the gang needed assurances."

He stopped talking as the waitress approached their table with Edward's coffee.

"Edward looked over his shoulder to make sure the waitress was gone. "Did you tell him we will prosecute his wife to the full capacity of the law and she will be going to prison for a long time?"

"Are you loco? You want me to threaten these guys? Absolutely not! We might be holding the cards right now, but don't forget, these guys can get to anybody and I still have family back in Mexico. Look, as much as I would be a beneficiary of John Rosenberg being at the governor's mansion in Annapolis, it's not worth getting my family killed over. If your boss doesn't like it, I could care less."

"Alright! Calm down. What do you suggest?"

"I think if you come with me to Petersburg to talk to Carlito, it will go a long way. These guys know very well that when the U.S Attorney's office is involved, you are serious. it will reinforce my credibility with them and nullify any fear or doubt they might have had, even without a legal document."

"What about the girl? Any update?"

"She is not a threat. She seems genuinely interested in helping her client out. She has visited the prison couple of times to see him, but it's no big deal. A lot of these rich kids from big law firms seem to feel guilty about the privileged life they've lived and would go beyond the call of duty to help guys like Danny Adeyinka to be free and become like them someday."

"What about all her visits to the U.S. attorney's office in the northern district?"

"Also, a dead end. She seems to be in love with an Assistant U.S. Attorney over there."

"Who?" asked Edward curiously.

"Some guy named Jonas Malone. You know him?"

"Yes. We worked together on couple of cases. What a loser! Oh well, I've got to get back to the office. I don't have the luxury of a field agent roaming the streets."

"So, when are we doing this?" asked Ramirez.

"I'll get back to you. I need to check in with the boss on these developments. Don't worry, the drinks are on me."

Edward paid for the drinks at the bar and walked out in a hurry to cross the street.

THE CHOW HALL WAS PACKED AND NOISY. Danny was enjoying a delicious turkey drumstick with mashed potatoes, gravy, string beans and broccoli. The meal was a gift from the warden in honor of Thanksgiving. Half-way through his meal, two officers approached Danny's table and asked him to stand up with his hands on his head. He was being arrested for possession of contrabands. The warden had given the order for a complete shake-down of all cells in every hall during dinner.

It was obvious to everyone that Danny was on his way to the hole. Couple of months before, Danny would have thrown a fit and resisted the arrest. Since becoming a Christian, he had learnt to trust God even when he felt violated and treated unjustly. Nevertheless, he still could not understand how they had found contrabands in his locker. As they walked him out of the chow hall, Danny thought of Carlito and the El-Rino gang and wondered if they had double-crossed him. Standing right by the entrance of the hall was Reggie, wearing an expression of disbelief. I'm sure he is thinking the same thing as I am, thought Danny.

The hole was empty. It felt like being in a dungeon. Danny could see Carlito Morales in the cell adjacent to his. He wasn't sure what to make of that development. He wondered how he would be able to call Lynn and Susan, since he would be on a twenty-three-hour lock-down and all phone privileges were automatically cut-off in solitary confinement. By now, officer Matthew and his posse would have packed up Danny's personal belongings from his cell and placed them in a secure room.

A couple of minutes later, Danny heard foot steps approaching his cell. His cell door opened, revealing a rather large man in a black suit.

"Good evening Mr. Adeyinka. I'm FBI Agent George Nowak. You can call me George. I'm in charge of the safety of you and Mr. Morales over there. At least, until after the investigation is over. I apologize for any inconveniences for arresting you in public view of most of the inmates."

"You are the reason I'm here?" asked Danny.

"Yes. It was a ruse and had to be done. We needed to get you and Mr. Morales into solitary confinement for your safety. It's come to our attention that agent Ramirez and the assistant U.S. Attorney, Edward Reese will be here on Monday to see Mr. Morales. From the brief I have, I heard this was your plan from the on-set. Impressive!"

"It's amazing what you can come up with when your life is being threatened and all you want to do is just survive. I'm curious though."

"What?" George said as if he was expecting the question.

"If you guys knew that they are coming on Monday as planned, why did you go through all this charade for our protection?"

"Good question, Mr. Adeyinka."

"You can call me Danny."

"Okay Danny. Even though we knew of their plans, we needed to consider the fact that they could approach the other gangs such as the Gambino crime family and the Nation of Islam to carryout out the same contract."

"Interesting! Did you guys have any intelligence or evidence backing that up? I'm just curious and not trying to tell you guys how to do your job."

"Nope, but we felt we didn't want to find out the hard way and I believe you don't object to being alive. Right?"

"Shoo! Can the Maasai in Kenya jump?"

"Sorry, who?" George asked with a confused look.

"Don't worry. I see you don't get it. The answer is yes."

"Alright. I've already briefed Mr. Morales. My colleague will be here in the morning to start his shift. It will please you to know that we arranged for another ration of the Thanksgiving dinner to be brought to you and Mr. Morales here in the hole. Do you have any other questions for me?"

"Nope. Just waiting for my grub. Thank you."

"I'll be in the officer's pod. Happy Thanksgiving Danny."

"Happy Thanksgiving George."

Danny could smell the roasted turkey heading his way. He waited by his bed patiently, listening to his stomach grumble.

Chapter 23

DANNY COULD HARDLY CATCH HIS BREATH. He had been doing push-ups for about an hour after breakfast. He believed in exercising whenever he was under pressure, especially when the weather was unforgiving as this morning. The floor and the walls of the cells were cold. He had not slept well. George and his colleagues were busy wiring the interview room with listening devices, planting bugs and cameras for total surveillance by the reception area. It must have around eleven o'clock, thought Danny when agent Novak walked Carlito Morales to reception. It had been interesting to see George dressed like a correction officer. He grabbed Carlito by his left arm, even though he was in handcuffs. Neither of them spoke as they walked by his cell. Everyone understood what was at stake and what roles they had to play to make it work. Since the whole plot had been Danny's idea, he felt frustrated having to take the back seat and wait to see how it all played out. To take his mind off whatever was going on in that interview room, he dropped back on the floor and started another round of push-ups.

Agent Ramirez and Edward Reese were already seated facing the door. George opened the door, shoved Carlito down on the seat and took off his handcuffs.

"That will be all officer. We'll take it from here", said agent Ramirez.

George hoped the wire on Carlito had not been affected by the way he'd shoved him down. He knew that If something was wrong, the agents listening in the adjacent room would signal to him. Nevertheless, George knew going back in the room was not an option. It would spook an experienced agent like Ramirez and that would blow the whole operation.

"Hey Carlito. I promised you I will be back, and you can count on me," said Ramirez.

"Who is this gringo you have with you?" Carlito asked.

"This is Mr. Edward Reese. He is a from the U.S. Attorney's office. He is the one who has the power to drop the charges against your wife and stop the USCIS from deporting her. When we spoke the last time I was here, you said you needed some assurances before you did anything."

"Yeah, but I told you I wanted it written down on a signed document specifying your request for me to either kill Danny Adeyinka and frame Reginald Beaufort for it or at least set him up against the B-More Boys to force him to testify against them in exchange for his safety."

Agent Novak has spent the weekend coaching Carlito to be aggressive about his demand and be frank about it. Nobody had to remind Carlito what to do. It was made clear on the agreement he signed with the northern district's U.S Attorney's office just a week before Thanksgiving. Martha had sent Jonas Malone to the prison with the document for Carlito to sign in the presence of his lawyer. The agreement had stated that a full confession from agent Ramirez and Edward Reese was necessary for the agreement to be honored.

Edward was uncomfortable with the way Carlito was openly discussing the specifics of their request, but calmed down when Ramirez reminded him they were in prison and not at the bureau. He told Edward, there is nothing to be worried about. The room is sound proof and very different to the interview room back at the bureau which was readily wired for interrogations. That made sense to Edward.

Edward raised his hands to stop Ramirez from responding and leaned forward to respond instead.

"Listen to me. Just as agent Ramirez told you earlier, my name is Edward Reese. I am the assistant U.S Attorney for the United States District Court. Everything agent Ramirez has told you is true. I would not be here if things were different. I have the power to drop the case against your wife and make the deportation order disappear. I'm sure there are some inmates here at Petersburg that I prosecuted. Why don't you ask them about me? They will tell you I don't play around."

"I've heard about you already," said Carlito massaging his ego just as agent Novak had coached him.

Edward felt invigorated and continued just as he had done in his closing arguments during court trials. "We need your help Carlito," he said calmly. "Reginald Beaufort is a very bad man and his release is getting closer by the day. Unless, we prosecute him and put him away, your wife will be in prison for a long time and your children will handed over to social welfare. I don't think I have to tell you what happens to kids in that system."

"Are you threatening me?" asked Carlito.

"No, I'm not. I'm just reminding you what is at stake here. Look, this is a good deal for you and the El-Rino gang. Your wife and your kids get to live in this country together as a family and El-Rino gang will also be able to get the major share of the city of Baltimore. We know you guys have been eying that city for a while."

"Okay, so what do you want me to do?" asked Carlito.

"Just like agent Ramirez told you already."

"No! I want to hear it from you. I need you to look me in the eye and tell me exactly what you need me to do. This way, I will know who to hold responsible just in case you renege."

"We won't renege", said Ramirez, afraid Reese might be terrified to do just that.

"Was I speaking to you, Ramirez? I want to hear it from him. That is the least he can do if he is not going to put it down on paper."

"Okay", said Edward. "We need you to get rid of Danny Adeyinka and frame Reginald Beaufort for it."

"You mean kill him?"

"Edward cleared his throat and said "yes."

"And if that doesn't work?"

"Then you can improvise by eliminating of one of the leaders of the B-More Boys and framing Danny Adeyinka, which will spark a call for reprisal."

"Eliminate?" asked Carlito.

"Okay, kill one of the leaders," said Edwards angrily. "Look that's it. Either you can, or we find someone else."

"Alright," said Carlito with both hands in the air. "I'll do it. Calm down. Just want to make sure there are no confusions."

Edward immediately stood up. "C'mon Ramirez, let's get out of here."

They banged on the door and agent Novak placed Carlito in handcuffs as they exited the room. Carlito could not wait to get back to his cell. He was elated. He had fulfilled his end of the agreement. There was a future for his wife and kids.

IT WAS BRIGHT AND SUNNY OUTSIDE when agent Ramirez and Edward Reese left the prison. They both walked towards the lock box where government officials and law enforcement officers were to place all electronic devices and firearms for safety purposes. Edward knew John would be excited to hear the plan was back on track and could not wait call his boss to deliver the news. Oblivious to the presence of the FBI agents, they were quickly surrounded.

"Edward Reese and Rodriguez Ramirez?"

"Yes. What's this and who are you?" asked Edward, surprised.

"I'm Agent George Novak of the Federal Bureau of Investigation. You and Agent Ramirez are under arrest for Conspiracy to Murder and Bribery of Public Officials and Witnesses. You have the right to remain silent. Anything you say can and will be used against you in a court of law. You have the right to an attorney. If you cannot afford an attorney, one will be provided for you. Do you understand the rights I have just read to you?"

"What? Do you know who I am? he shouted as they were both being handcuffed. I'm the assistant U.S. attorney for the Greenbelt division, southern district of Maryland."

"I know exactly who you are," replied George as he stepped in his face. "You make me sick. People like you are the reason the public has lost trust in our justice system." Get them out of here."

George was relieved. The operation had been successful. To secure the safety of his men, he had ordered their immediate arrest before Agent Ramirez could secure his weapon from the lockbox. Though he did not anticipate any resistance, he could not afford to risk it. There was a lot riding on this. He picked up his phone and called Martha.

Chapter 24

MARTHA STOOD OUTSIDE THE INTERVIEW ROOM IN THE BASEMENT LEVEL of the courthouse looking through the two-way mirror at agent Ramirez. The man sat with his hands covering his face. She had an idea of how he must have been feeling, sitting on the opposite side of the table where he had been the interrogator for hundreds of cases, closing in on a perpetrator, armed with a barrage of evidence for leverage to draw out a confession.

In her own way, she felt pity for him. She hoped she would never end up on the other side of that table. However, she had a job to do and had decided to offer agent Ramirez a deal to corroborate all the evidence they had to present an air tight case against her colleague in the Southern District whose father was a powerful Senator and Chairman of the Judiciary Committee. Martha knew that the Rosenberg family would not go down without a fight; they would wield all their political muscle to protect themselves.

The attorney-general was ready to protect himself and throw her under the bus if this went sideways. As an experienced prosecutor, she understood Ramirez was the weaker link and would be the best person to leverage. He had a lot to lose with a long list of abuse allegations. He came from a poor background and was easily dispensable. She had no doubt, he would cooperate.

"Hello, Ramirez. My name is Martha Jenkins."

"I know who you are, he said. Why don't you get to the point and get it over with? I've sat in that seat where you are for over two decades, so I can see you coming a mile away. What are you offering?"

"Would you like your lawyer to be present for this interview?"

"No. I can handle myself. Like I said, what are you offering?"

"You are charged with two counts of felonies. First, Conspiracy to Murder under Title 18 U.S. Code 1117 which carries a maximum sentence of life imprisonment. Secondly, Bribery of Public Officials and Witnesses under Title 18 U.S. Code which carries a maximum sentence of two years. We need you to cooperate and testify against Edward Reese and John Rosenberg, stating the role you played from the onset of this conspiracy down to the last detail. If you cooperate, we are offering a sentence of six months on both counts to run concurrently. This is the best you are going to get and there is one-hour time limit on this deal."

"I need immunity. What about my job and my pension?"

"Are you kidding?" said Martha. "For a case of this magnitude? Not a chance! Everyone is going to do some jail time. Your days as an agent are over. The Secret Service will be terminating your service with immediate effect. You should count yourself lucky. You still get to keep your pension. I'm being generous here and you should take advantage of it."

"No, you're not? We both know you need me as a witness to seal the conviction you need to prosecute this case successfully. So, you can stop the pretense of being nice."

"Personally, I don't give a crap. Do we have a deal or not?"

"Sure, we do. Now, I need my lawyer. Just curious, how long have you guys been on us?"

"Just before your meeting with Edward Reese at the café. It's amazing how useful those sugar shakers can be when you need one," she said with a smirk as she exited the room.

He banged his fist on the table. How could he have been so careless? Then he started laughing hysterically, knowing the fate of Edward Reese and John Rosenberg was sealed.

Danny woke up earlier than usual for his morning prayer and devotion. He was feeling great. Danny had achieved the final part of his plan when he called Lynn to propose to her. He had been less nervous waiting to hear if Carlito was successful. Lynn picked up the phone and sounded relived and excited. She was happy that the whole saga was over.

"Hi sweetie," she said. "Glad you called. I've been waiting to hear your voice."

"Me too dear. Just got a few minutes to talk. I need to tell you something."

"What's wrong?" she asked, nervously.

"Nothing is wrong. No worries."

"Danny Adeyinka, you better be straight with me. I can hear you breathing. Spit it out."

"Would you marry me?" Danny blurted.

The phone went silent for couple of seconds. It felt like eternity to Danny.

Lynn screamed. Danny moved the receiver away from his ears.

"Yes, Yes, Yes, she said excited. I will marry you Danny. I thought you'd never ask."

"I don't have anything to give you now dear, but I promise to love you all the days of my life."

"I just want you, Danny. I love you."

"Love you too. We'll talk more when you come to visit. Good night."

Danny hung up. He went back to his bunk grinning with a spring in his step.

Danny had been in the hole for almost a month now. The warden had asked if Danny was ready to go back into the prison population after John Rosenberg was arrested two weeks ago, but he said no. He had just two weeks left on his sentence and wanted to leave in peace, even though he had been elevated to a rock star status.

No inmate in the history of Petersburg Prison and its environs had been successful in taking down a United States Attorney. It had been all over the news when John was arrested. He had been giving a speech at a criminal justice conference in D.C when the FBI stormed into the building and arrested him right in front of all his esteemed colleagues. Danny saw the spring in George Novak's step, as he walked ahead of his team to approach the podium where John Rosenberg was making his presentation. Someone had alerted the media and the paparazzi had arrived at the building even before the FBI could walk John into the waiting cruiser. It was a media sensation and breaking news on all cable channels. Even Fox News had to get in on the action, despite this being an embarrassment to the top brass of the Republican Party.

Susan had paid him a visit yesterday. It was a sweet and sour moment for Danny. He had become close to Susan over the past months and was sad not knowing when they would meet again. Susan had hoped Danny could have gotten a deal to avert his deportation out of this mess, but she knew better. Martha Jenkins already had her golden goose in Carlito Morales.

Nevertheless, Danny reminded Susan that he had gotten the best part of the deal by staying alive and getting his freedom in two weeks. In a way, Danny was looking forward to going home. He missed his family. He had spoken to the General and Evelyn two days ago to let them know approximately when he'd be arriving in Lagos. The U.S. Marshals had not been forth coming about the itinerary of the trip, since he was going to be on the plane with other convicts and deportees. They claimed it was for security reasons. He had just finished shining his boots, when he heard Reggie Beaufort's voice.

"Hello Danny? You are looking sharp. I see you are excited in anticipation of a visit from your fiancée."

"How did you know? Never mind", said Danny as he continued shining his boots.

"A little birdie told me that she just arrived at the visitor's hall. Just wanted to come and say a quick goodbye before you get released."

"Is that why you creeped over here? Can't we meet like normal people do?"

"Nope. You are not normal. You are Danny Adeyinka and this is how it's going to be. I've got a reputation to protect," he said laughing. "Jokes aside, I really want to thank you from the bottom of my heart. I owe you one."

"In that case, can I ask for a favor?"

"Name it."

"Would you consider giving up this gangster life, surrender your life to Christ and repenting of your ways? I can assure, you will not regret it. The way you are going, you might not survive the next ten years."

"Wait a minute! Is Danny Adeyinka worried about me?" Reggie teased.

Call it whatever you want. Just remember God loves you bro, and I love you too.

"For you? I'll think about it."

The officer in charge of the hole yelled from the entrance, "You have a visitor, Danny."

"C'mon, I'll walk you out," said Reggie.

As usual, Lynn did not disappoint. Dressed in a blue cashmere blouse over a plaid skirt and high heeled boots, she looked gorgeous. Danny could not hide his excitement. This was the first time they had seen each other face to face since he had proposed to her over the phone after John Rosenberg's arrest. He gave her a tight hug and a kiss. She was crying.

"Hey, what's wrong? I thought you would be happy since I'm about to be released in two weeks, and let's not forget that I'm still alive. All in one piece."

"I love you Danny and I'm happy. Though you are getting released, you are still getting deported. What's going to happen to us?"

"Don't worry about that. Let's take it one step at a time," he said as he held her hands. "The world is bigger than the United States. We can get married in Nigeria. What do you think?"

"Maybe Danny. I've never left the shores of the U.S. and I don't even have a passport. However, my desire is to get married before you leave, even if it means getting married right here in Petersburg Prison."

"I don't think illegal aliens can get married here. They frown on such request because they think it's a ploy to avert a deportation order."

"Well, I'm not giving up, she said angrily. I'll call the warden and make my case, even if I must get the media involved. I don't think he would want to deny my request after what just happened with you. After all, you are Danny Adeyinka."

"Yes ma'am", said Danny saluting her. He knew not to argue. She deserved whatever her heart desired.

PRESENT DAY

Chapter 25

IT'S BEEN FIVE YEARS SINCE DANNY LANDED ON THE SHORES OF NIGERIA. He had succeeded in getting married at Petersburg Prison a week before his release. It was an exquisite event. Family members could attend, and Dexter was honored to be the best man.

Lynn arrived at the Federal Capital Territory, Abuja two weeks after Danny was deported. Evelyn had arranged a nice three-bedroom apartment in the posh area of the city for them. She wanted to make sure they were both comfortable, especially Lynn, since this was her first time living abroad. A few weeks later, Lynn got a job as a teacher at the American International School. Danny was grateful to God and counted his blessings.

Danny slept like a baby last night and was woken by the sound of the rooster crowing. He was due to address the Nigerian Senate Judiciary Committee in conjunction with other stakeholders in the polity. Susan Macarthy was scheduled as a keynote speaker. She had been nominated as a United Nation Ambassador for Human Rights six months after John Rosenberg and Edward Reese were each sentenced to five years in prison on a plea deal. Danny and Lynn had spent the previous night with her at the Sheraton Hotel reminiscing about old times.

"Can I see your ring?" Lynn asked Susan. "It's so beautiful. Sorry, we couldn't make it to your wedding. As you know, Danny has been barred indefinitely from the United States."

"Well, you guys are forgiven", Susan said, laughing.

"So, how is Jonas Malone? I heard he is now the U.S. Attorney for the northern district of Maryland."

"Yes, he is. He was appointed and confirmed by the President, and Martha Jenkins, who is now the new U.S. Attorney-General. At the speed she is going, I won't be surprised if she runs in the next presidential election. As for Jonas, he hopes to retire five years from now. He wants to make up for all the lost times and enjoy life."

"I agree. Please send our regards", said Danny.

"Did you hear about Reginald Beaufort?" said Susan. "So sad."

"Nope. I've not heard from him since we last spoke when I was in the hole."

"He was murdered in St Louis, two years after his release. He was found at an upscale hotel, shot in the back of the head. An assassination, I'll say."

"Do they know who was responsible?"

"No. Nobody has claimed responsibility for it and there has not been any arrest either."

The U.S government would not lose any sleep over Reggie's death," Danny reasoned. He hoped he'd given his life to Christ before he died.

Danny waited for Lynn as she got ready to head to school. He sat at the table reading the newspapers, eagerly going through the front page of *The Guardian*.

"EXXODUS Challenging the Federal Government on Human Rights Abuses of Inmates in the Nigerian Prisons."

As the executive director of Exxodus, a non-profit organization he founded, Danny had made a pledge to fight for those being abused by public servants and government officials. He was appalled at the state of the criminal justice system where the rule of law was non-existent and there was no regard for human rights.

"Are you ready?" yelled Lynn coming out of the bedroom. "I don't want to be late for school. I have couple of meetings with parents."

"I'm ready", he said grabbing his jacket. It was sunny and clear. A light breeze blew among beautiful flowers scattered around the front lawn. Danny took a deep breath and got into the driver's seat, Lynn sat next to him adjusting the mirror on the visor for last minute touch-up on her lipstick.

"You look beautiful dear," said Danny.

"Thank you honey," she said. She kissed him. "May God allow the committee to adopt the proposal you are presenting today."

"Amen. I am confident they will. I already prayed about it. They can't afford to ignore us. At least, not on my watch."

They drove into town and headed towards the city center.

ABOOKS

ALIVE Book Publishing and ALIVE Publishing Group
are imprints of Advanced Publishing LLC,
3200 A Danville Blvd., Suite 204, Alamo, California 94507

Telephone: 925.837.7303 Fax: 925.837.6951
www.alivebookpublishing.com